W9-AQR-267

An Agreement
Between Us

An Agreement Between Us

Stories by John Hermann

A BREAKTHROUGH BOOK

UNIVERSITY OF
MISSOURI PRESS

ACKNOWLEDGMENTS

"Shebie" was originally published in *Perspective*,
Winter, 1972, and is included in this collection
by permission of Perspective.

"Penates" was originally published in *The
Virginia Quarterly Review*, Spring, 1968, and
is included in this collection by permission of
The Virginia Quarterly Review.

"The Piranha" was originally published in *Northwest
Review*, Vol. IV, No. 2 (Spring, 1961), and is
included in this collection by permission of Northwest Review.

"Akroterion" was originally published in *Pyramid*, #12
(1971), copyright 1972 by Hellric Publications. It is included in this collection by permission
of Hellric Publications.

"Due Process" was originally published in the Winter,
1971, issue of *Descant* and is included in this
collection by permission of the Texas Christian
University Press.

ISBN 0–8262–0140–7 *Paper*
ISBN 0–8262–0141–5 *Cloth*
Library of Congress Catalog Number 72–95437
Printed in the United States of America

To Margot

Contents

Shebie

It is simple enough. Now, forty–five years later, one of my better tennis shots is a pick–up, top–spin drive off my forehand that I mastered when I was eight because the baseline of the tennis court was a foot away from the chickenwire backstop that separated the court from Mrs. Ceronsky's vegetable garden.

Because at that time there were no tennis courts in town—9,632 left–over lumbermen and railroad workers in northern Wisconsin: Gunkel the baker who sold his rye bread to Novotony the shoeman who sold his hunting boots to Molle the jeweller who sold Gunkel the gold watch that told when Novotony's bread was done in the oven. So we kids made our own beyond Heinie Duchac's backyard fence where his father used to have his coal and lumber business. But every time we dragged the court and watered it and marked it with lime, the lumps of coal kept coming to the surface like shells washed up on a beach. Except for Shorty Lingle, we even strung our own rackets. Somewhere out of the foaming beer money of his father's tavern business, he emerged down the rickety stairs of his second–story apartment with a steel racket which he used with such left–handed dexterity in cuts and spins that he outclassed all of us—even my older brother. It was on the court, my back against the chickenwire fence, that my pick–ups were perfected. Of such carrot and radish rows of aberrations in Mrs. Ceronsky's garden am I fashioned like a rock in a riverbed. Cuneiform note: I haven't eaten cucumbers since the ones I stole with my brother from Griffith's backyard. Sliced with our pocketknives and eaten, they flattened me in the field of hay beyond our fence, where on my back, hidden from my mother, I fought down the waves of vomit pumping upward in my throat.

Those are some of the illusions in any case, as if the compost of those days could be assessed by what birch and maple and elm leaves fell each year in the woods at Sugar Bush where with our parents my brother and I went every spring to pick flowers for May baskets—violets, trilliums, jack–in–the–pulpits? The flowers hang like framed, oval memories in my mind. The May baskets, cone–shaped, made out of colored papers to be hung on the doorknobs of neighbors' houses? Cousin Maymie's? Uncle Josie's? Can that be true? Am I making that up? What mother fancying in May must that have been which if true had my father backing our Model T from the garage past the flower boxes in front of the bay window, past the peonies beside the driveway, and into the shade of our box–elder street?

So, too, out of those leaf–mold days came: Shebie, a motorcycle policeman who as far as I knew was the only law officer in town. His real name was Shibuski, I think, and I never saw him arrest anyone in the seventeen years I stayed there, before the Depression drove me out of that tie–plug–factory, lasts–for–shoes land, and I never returned. His motorcycle had a blue–gold insignia on the side of the gasoline tank, and an isinglass shield in front of the speedometer. He carried a notebook in his shirt pocket so small it looked like a miniature Bible, and in it he jotted down names and complaints and addresses—the criminals of the town, I imagined.

On the Fourth of July he propped his cycle on its kickstand beneath the clock of the First National Bank and directed the parade down Main Street. In the winter he disappeared as if, like my father with our Model T, he had taken the wheels off his motorcycle and put it up on blocks until the first thaw in April. He was as predictable as the seasons: we could grab an armful of pea–vines from a wagonload going through the streets to the canning factory at the edge of town, but if we broke old man Boll's window while playing ball back of Gibbonses' barn and then ran like marbles scattering across a porch, he'd gather us all together, knowing where we lived, and say: "All right now. Mr. Boll will get the window fixed and give me the bill, which should be about a buck and a quarter, and I want (let's see, five, six of you) twenty cents from each one when I come around Friday."

"Okay," my brother says, "I'll get it collected," appointing himself special deputy.

Somewhere out of the tangle of pea–vines in our laps in the garage as we flopped them over to find the pods we had missed, out of the sound of tinkling glass as a punt bounded through a kitchen window, Shebie emerged, as if in his black book he were the monitor of our moralities more than old Father Kolby was who, marinated in wine and incense, you got a whiff of, everytime you got near.

Viz:

Wil James, a high school kid who lived as a kind of handyman two doors down with Mrs. Hartford, hanged himself in the basement, and my mother cut him down. She comes running around the corner of Grall's house toward home, her arms upraised, screaming I can't understand what, past me, and up the front porch of our house. "Police . . . call the police," I think she is saying. Screendoors slam up and down the block, and Mrs. Ceronsky in a flowered apron comes running along the sidewalk, and Mrs. Gunkel across the street comes out to her front porch, and because all the men are at work, only Mr. Unger, deaf and an idiot (my mother says) comes waddling, rake in hand, across the street. A crowd gathers, standing in Grall's driveway looking at the basement window behind which we know Wil James has been hanging until my mother found him. I see him there crumpled in the gloom next to the shelves of Mason jars—beets, carrots, blueberries. I can hear my mother on the phone in our house calling the operator, banging the receiver up and down, her voice a babble, and beyond that the opening of Marie Basel's backdoor as she too will be coming around the line of hollyhocks, up our driveway, to see what has happened that she didn't know about and other people did. But before my mother bloated with hysteria like a poisoned potato bug can emerge from the front door again, I hear Shebie's motorcycle turning off Main Street into the box-elder shade of Edison and can see him as he crosses Sixth Avenue, and then he has turned his motorcycle into Grall's driveway among us, canted its wheel, shoved the bike up on its kickstand, and the talking subsides. He stops briefly to talk with Mrs. Gunkel who points to the kitchen door, and I imagine she says: "Downstairs. In the cellar. The steps are in the kitchen." But he hardly stops in his striding—up the back porch, through the door, and disappears.

I am hip–pocket high, so that I see everything between pantlegs, beyond the rickrack of aprons, shunted aside with a hand on my shoulder, stepped in front of. I go to stand beside the wheel of Shebie's motorcycle, beside the ordered treads of that front tire's authority, and watch. My mother comes back from our house running, saying, "I think he's alive. I cut him down but he was still breathing. I think he's alive . . . ," but they stop her as if by design—a cluster of Mrs. Basel, Sengstock, Grall, Gunkel—reaching out an arm to keep her from rushing into the cellar again: "Shebie's down . . . ," and she stops and joins them, her words pouring out in gasps like water from a pump. She is not my mother. She is a woman with hair sprung upward like the padding from a cracked car–seat, until Shebie emerges again through the door, onto the porch, his hat in his hand like a mourner, it seems to me, although it may have been just hot down there in that musty basement bending over Wil James's body. (It is the first I know that he is bald, the whiteness sitting like a plate, the edges that clear, on the top of his head.) As he comes down the porch steps, my mother is already next to him. "He's alive, isn't he? I cut him down in time, didn't I?" The words tumble over each other like potatoes pouring from a crate.

Shebie stops a moment, and I can hear him say with what I take is sadness: "No, Mrs. Schmitz. He's dead." He comes to his bike, and when he turns to take something from a clipboard behind the isinglass visor, I see that the cord on the seat of his trousers is as shiny as that of my last year's school pants. He turns to where Mrs. Grall and Marie Basel and Mrs. Brismaster are knotted together talking and says, "Can I use your phone, Mrs. Grall?"

She turns her head. "It's in the dining room, Shebie, next to the staircase." The blue–black trousers go, and I am left to guard his bike.

When he returns and goes to stand by the steps of the back porch, the whole neighborhood has gathered, even Malaria Pollak, the girl my age next door, who has come to stand beside me. "Wil James hung himself," I tell her. "My mother cut him down."

"Where?" she says as if she would see him hanging. I point to the basement window, dusty, pock-marked with rain, gutter–spattered from long ago. "Right there," I say. My voice is full of authority like that of my mother who is telling the story once again to Mrs. Siesel who has joined the group: ". . . and I ran upstairs for her paring knife, and . . . ." Her voice rises like a bird among the leaves of the box elders, until Muttart's undertaker car backs into the driveway, directed by Shebie. Mr. Muttart and Shebie take a long wicker basket with a lid like a mummy case up the porch steps, through the open screen door. When they come out again, the basket sags like a hammock from the handles with the weight of Wil James's body. They rest the basket a moment in the driveway in front of Malaria and me—Wil James there, a rope around his neck—while they open the back doors of the car. They lift the basket up again, Mr. Muttart on one side, Shebie on the other, and slide it into the back of the car.

After the doors are closed and the car has left, it is Shebie who goes and detaches my mother with a hand on her arm from the knot of women and tells her: "You better come home and get some rest now, Mrs. Schmitz," as he leads her along the sidewalk toward our house. As they pass me, I can hear her telling him: "I cut him down, Shebie, as soon as I could."

"I know you did, Mrs. Schmitz," he says, his hat in his hand as he takes her up the front steps of our house. "You did all you could."

Or:

My brother and Fatty Donahue and I have just finished a two–story shack in Donahue's backyard, made out of the old piano boxes we get from behind Barney Jewel's Music Store. We are planning a cook–out—a stew. Just where the meat has come from or the black, iron kettle my brother has in front of him between his crossed legs as he sits in the backyard, I do not remember. It is mid–afternoon, when the lace curtains are drawn across the neighbors' windows to protect the ferns, like my mother's, growing in baskets inside; when the clusters of maple seeds that look like waterwings hang motionless over the sidewalks. It is in that afternoon somnolence that my brother dispatches Fatty and me to Shapek's garden that stretches behind the house next door to get some green onions. It is no time to be stealing from a vegetable garden in full sight of Mrs. Siesel, the back–door neighbor, who has only to look up from scrubbing her kitchen sink to see, beyond her apple orchard, what we are doing.

We complain but we go, slipping behind Shapek's garage and along the barbed–wire fence of the garden, pretending we are going to get Nonny Gibbons for a ballgame. Once out of sight, we duck through the fence, and each of us in fistfulls of grabbing decimates the end of an onion row. We stuff the onions, green tops and all, within our shirts. For some reason, now inexplicable, I am wearing a satin, blue blouse that my mother has remade from one of Art Oelke's worn-out shirts (a richer, Milwaukee cousin). It is one of my best, and as I stuff the onions through my open shirt front, a wet smudge of dirt clinging around the onions smears the open buttonhole. Fatty's shirt, too, bulges. We stop behind the garage to adjust the onions around our waistbands. It is then that Nora Shapek, the spinster daughter of the old lady, comes around the corner of the garage.

"What are you boys doing?" she says, and coming

up to me (the hand, the finger, as fastidious as if she is touching a dead crawdad), she pulls wider my open shirt front, where, looking down, I see the onions lying in the pale blue light inside my shirt. "And you, James," she says to Fatty Donahue as if by being her neighbor his crime is even more shocking than mine.

One on each side, a hand around our arm, hunching up our shoulders, she marches us toward the house, past my brother on the other side of the driveway who sits beside the shack, the kettle between his crossed legs. He looks at us as if we were some backwoods moonshiners from Kopenich he has never seen before, brought into town for the first time by the sheriff. "He . . ." I begin to say, but without stopping, we are marched through the back door into the kitchen where old Mrs. Shapek stands, dressed in black, her hand like a warty gourd resting on a cane.

Both Fatty and I have taken the onions from our shirt fronts, and we stand before her with the onions like a bouquet of flowers in our hands, the snapped, hollow stems bent over in defeat. She says nothing. Her eyes from the grey wrinkled newspaper of her face, however, have the glint of cupidity as if she has finally caught all those fish who have for so long nibbled at her line, grabbing the bait and never getting caught until now. Nora releases us before her mother. "I found them coming around the corner of the garage," she says as if identifying us before a magistrate.

"Send that one home," the mother says, leaning her cane, the end still on the floor, in Fatty's direction. She doesn't even look at him. "I'll talk with his mother later." Fatty starts to leave. "Put the onions on the table, young man," she says as he reaches the door, and Fatty comes back and puts the fistful of onions on the porcelain top of the kitchen table and leaves.

"Who's this one?" she says. I hear the backdoor close as Fatty goes outside, and I am left alone with the two women in the house, its windows shrouded with net curtains like spider webs.

"He's Mrs. Schmitz's boy. On Edison, I think," Nora says.

The old lady looks at me. "Is that right?"

"Yes'm."

"You can put your onions on the table too," she says and turns toward the dining room. I put my onions beside Fatty's on the table, wipe my hand on my pants leg, button up my shirt. Outside, far away, my brother sits in the sunshine with a kettle between his legs. Damn him. Nora nudges me toward the other room, a herded sheep. The old lady has gone to the telephone on the sideboard. A fern like my mother's fills a bay window. The tablecloth is a crocheted, circular pattern. There are doilies everywhere—under vases, on end tables. The old lady is paging through the telephone book.

"Call the jail," Nora says. "Call Mr. Shibuski."

The old lady doesn't answer. Beyond the fern, beyond the lace curtain, I can see the edge of our shack next door back of Fatty's house. "Is your father's name Karl?" the old lady says, and I turn back to where she has a finger stick–pinning a name like a butterfly on the open page of the directory.

"Yes'm," I say.

"And what's your name?"

"Ubi," I say.

She repeats it: "Ubi? That's not your real name," she says.

"No, ma'am."

"What does your mother call you?"

"William," I say.

She takes the receiver from its hook and waits. "Operator? Get me Y–673, please."

But it is our house, not Shebie.

Except:

At fifty, I know enough not to camp, pulling tight the guy ropes of a tent, zipping shut the netting to keep out the mosquitoes at night, blowing up an air mattress so my hipbones won't be sore in the morning. I know it, but my wife wants to verify the poster–colored seas pasted on the brochures from Hawaii.

"But . . . ," I begin to say when she suggests it.

"We can camp," she says as if granting me a concession.

"How old do you think I am?"

"You're fifty–three," she says.

We spend two weeks on the Big Island, I in my hammock beneath the kiawe trees at Hapuna Beach, a cove of curving sand where the breakers in mother–swells lift me, floating, toward the sky, and where the sun in the evening, like a monstrance over the water, draws everyone, even us, like a magnet to sit cross–legged, silent, on the beach. We are the grandparents of the campground, the young around us in other tent-ings. Silhouetted against the grey–purple dusk, they move in rituals—adding a stick of wood to their fires, carrying a bucket of water back to their campsites.

At the end of a week I am practicing a Renaissance song on a borrowed recorder. There is no mirror to show back the whiteness of my beard, no barber to bother the hair growing over my ears. Cathy in the distance walking toward the down–toppling foam of an incoming wave as she goes swimming, has slimmed to a girlhood of grace. In the mornings the undeco-rated dawn comes through the branches of the trees, and without pretense a roach admits to fright as it scuttles and scrambles over the bottom of our food box as I get out my breakfast egg.

"Well?" Cathy says as if proving a point, and in answer I send Fatty Donahue up the draw of tangled kiawe trees back of our tent to find out where the enemy could be.

At the end of two weeks I knock down the tent, exchange my swimming trunks for a pair of slacks, and we fly to Maui, where two women secretaries in the county office that gives out camping permits look at us as we enter the door as if we have invaded their living room.

The younger secretary is talking to someone at the counter: "Camp only in this place at Kalama. And at Makena only here. The police will have a record of where you are . . . ." Cathy takes her place in line. I sit down on one of the vacant secretary chairs. At her desk, the other secretary in a girdle and conical bra outlines her lips in the mirror–compact held over the top of her typewriter, makes them fuller as if advertising her generosity. It fools no one.

When it is Cathy's turn, she answers the questions fed to her, computer quick, while the data is written down in triplicate: "Where will you be camping? How long? How many? Just you and your husband? Tent? Camper? When do you plan to leave?"

Cathy turns to me holding the map of Maui in my hand as if I were helping. "What does it say there . . . the name of that campground . . . where?"

"It says," I pretend to read from the map, "we are mad." The secretary doing her lips snaps shut her compact. She has experienced haoles before. Cathy takes the map from my hand.

"That campground, that one there," she says to the girl, her finger attached to a place on the edge of the island where words like Krawakapu, Puu Olai, like the spikes of a sea urchin, extend into the blue of the ocean.

The girl cocks her head sideways to read the name. "Kalama," she says and writes it down on her sheet. "You'll be there Tuesday, the 17th, right?"

Cathy looks at me.

"Do as the girl says."

"Yes," Cathy says to the girl.

We are given the triplicate, pink. I fold it and put it in my wallet.

"At Kalama," the girl explains, "your tent must be between Pavilion #12 and the caretaker's house . . ."

"Where's that?" I say.

". . . no place else. And at Hana . . ." She turns, hesitant, to the other secretary who is putting a carbon between Form 202919 (I imagine) which is resting on the paten sanctity of her desk.

"Just in the compound itself"; the voice is already weary with the untidiness that each morning washes up against the back edge of her desk. I swing my chair, my mocasins, in her direction, as if interested in what she is saying, the stubble of my beard held like an icon above the barricade of her typewriter. She pays no attention.

"Just in the compound at Hana," the other girl tells my wife as she files one copy of the permit in a basket on the counter. "The other goes to the police." It is supposed to be a warning. Other campers have come in, stand in line, wait. We are sandaled, barefooted, bearded, carrying bedrolls which we prop against the counter, against the secretary's desk. Cathy and I leave, saying hello to the husband and wife in line (she with a baby in a backpack) that we have met at Hapuna.

"Get out your dogtags," I tell the white teeth and black beard of the husband as I pass.

He smiles. "36262928."

The girl at the counter is already inserting the carbon into another triplicate for the next couple: "Where will you be camping? How long? The police . . ."

We camp at Kalama, pitching our tent between the end of Pavilion #12 and the caretaker's house. The campground is a park, walled–in, waist–high, between the road and the beach, with some coconut trees and with a line of picnic pavilions on the edge of the sand. When we arrive, a few tents, a makeshift tarp or two strung between trees, are scattered over the campsite. I pick out a group of trees where the clusters of coconuts have already been knocked down. I want none of them bounding onto our tent when the winds begin. Ten yards away near the stone wall that separates the campground from the road, a girl with long swatches of hair falling in front of her face sits cross–legged on an open sleeping bag playing with a baby, five–, six–months old, naked. Its crying is an in–out, in–out, in–out whine. Behind her, over a rope between two trees, is a plastic triangle for a tent. Rocks hold down the corners. A canvas army pack leans against one of the trees. She is wearing a kind of mother–hubbard shift of a flour–sack print with spaghetti straps to hold it up. Her voice is a monotone babbling beside the baby's crying. I pound in the stakes of our tent with the section of waterpipe I have sawed off and brought along because I couldn't find my mallet, and when I come around the front guy rope to the other side, looking up, I see she is watching. I smile as does she from a face that is a mushy melon of uncertain flesh.

That evening, after the campground has filled up with hitchhiking kids from the road, with a group of high school bicyclers from New York and Philadelphia whose packs tumbled on the ground from the back of their bikes have the precision folds of a parachute; after I have scrubbed my hibachi with sand to get off the grease of our steak grilling, Cathy meets her in the washroom and comes back with the story.

We discuss it in our sleeping bags in the tent that night, the nylon tent–top stretching over us still orange in the diminishing light. Outside I hear the gush of water from a faucet, the call of someone from the beach, the cough of the baby, as the camp settles down.

"She's from San Francisco," Cathy says, "and she's run out of her welfare money."

My air mattress has the buoyancy of a breaker. Hands behind my head, I float out to sea, her voice a murmur turned toward me.

"The police have been kicking them out of one campground after another." Her words have the urgency edge of a mother. She could be talking about our own daughter who has just tried out a commune in Questo.

"She'll be all right," I say. "Who's the guy hanging around? That her husband?" It isn't the word, but it is the best I can manage for the interchangeable boys who follow the girl like stray dogs.

"He hasn't any money either," she says, "and they don't even have soap for the diapers."

"Let's see in the morning," I say. The sound of the foam gushing onto the shore comes from the direction of the beach, and I slide outward with the receding wave. As I go to sleep, Cathy, still talking, is a warmth in the darkness on the raft beside me.

At dawn, the sun through the orange, nylon top lights up our tent like a temple. Cathy is still asleep. Outside, the whine of the baby uncurls like a petal against the noise of the ocean. A pan knocks against the water faucet near the pavilion. A truck goes past on the road. I awake again in Aunt Annie's farmhouse at Sugar Bush, my toes warm in the bottom of the bed, while downstairs the screendoor bangs in the kitchen; outside, the windmill creaks and the water from the pipe mouth plunges into the drinking trough for the horses. In from the window comes the moo–oo–ing of a cow, and I imagine the upstretched muzzle and the line of Holsteins going along the fence from the barn out to pasture. My brother is a huddle of patchwork quilt beside me.

I crawl out to an opalescence that, over the ocean, is polishing the coiling scoop of the waves. The blue tent that has been near the washhouse is already gone. Beneath a tree, ten yards away, a girl with an Indian headband holding back her shoulder–length hair is on her knees rolling up her sleeping bag as tight as a log. The rest of her pack leans against the tree trunk. The hands, the slim wrists, are those of my daughter. The baby has stopped crying. I turn to where the mother sits, cross–legged, nursing it outside the triangle of her tent. Her sullen face, bent, is bathed in a Vermeer window–light. The grill of my hibachi beside the flap of our tent still smells of the steak. I take my towel, my washcloth from where they hang over the end of my hammock and go toward the washhouse, stepping around the sleeping bags—an upraised elbow, a tumble of waterfall hair. I circle the bare back of swimming trunks squatted beside a token fire that is being fed with sticks. It is an agreement between us, ten, fifteen yards apart, to pretend in each other's privacy, the contiguity that of an army, and even though the fifty–year old muscle of my calf is stiff in the morning chill, my mocasins, behind Boogie Gibbons's barn, are still slightly pigeon-toed as I walk across the grass.

Later, while I knock down the tent, getting ready

to move to Hana as our pink slip tells us to do, Cathy goes over and talks with the girl. When she returns, she says, daring me to disagree, "I'm going to give her the rest of our eggs and bread."

"Why don't you?" I say. I am prying up the stakes with the open end of my lead pipe, tossing them in a pile at the base of a coconut tree.

She fumbles through the food box, taking out the egg carton, the bread, the jar of peanut butter. "These too," she says.

"That's fine," I say as I unknot the guy lines that fasten the top of the tent to the tree trunk.

She carries the food toward where the baby on its stomach, its bare ass red with rash, is kicking its legs, waving its hands, on the sleeping bag beside its mother.

In the car, our stuff stowed away, Cathy beside me on the way to Hana wears the aura of a ruffled hen. "That girl is *so* simple . . ."

"We all are." I make it into a joke.

". . . nobody even knows where she is, so how is she to get her welfare check even if it is sent from San Francisco. Live in the Banana Patch. God, how stupid."

On the road ahead of us, the girl I have seen rolling her pack that morning has been stopped by a policeman, his car parked on the other side of the road. He has the conical hat of a forest ranger. She is answering a question, her head nodding back toward the campground we have just left.

"Isn't she the girl . . . ," Cathy says as we pass.

In the rear–view mirror, I see the girl take out something from her shirt pocket and show it to the policeman. The road turns, and the two of them disappear behind the bulge of a tree.

"Yes, it is," I say.

The road to Hana, the Amalfi drive of the islands some brochure had said, is a pot–holed quagmire that cows would have stumbled on, and when we do get to Hana, to the campground there beside the ocean, the rain hangs like a beaded curtain between us and the end of the pier. A VW camper parked there looks like a turtle, all its windows and doors tightened shut. Between the road and the beach there is a single pavilion, and the campground, a picnic park with two green tables, is deserted. I park the car, and through the rain we watch the grey waves pile into the rocks of the shore in an arm–weary lashing whose purpose has been forgotten.

"At Hana, camp anyplace." I quote the secretary from the office.

When the rain abates, a man, the caretaker I presume, comes toward the car from a building across the road. I roll down the window as he approaches. A Japanese, he has the billcap and T-shirt of a coach. "You people planning to camp here?"

"We thought so."

"The camp is closed," he says. The regular features are almost handsome—the mouth a line, the nose straight, the eyes nonexistent behind dark glasses.

"The county office . . ."

"It's closed," he says. "There's been too many of these kids around here. With hepatitis." The voice is frayed with anger as if some kids carrying bedrolls had just bombed out, with B-52's, the whole side of his island.

"The county office . . . ," I begin again, and Cathy shoves the pink permit she has taken from her purse into my hand.

"The campground is closed," he says and walks back across the road toward his office.

I roll up the window.

"We've got a permit," Cathy says.

"You heard the man," I tell her. The rain begins again, bouncing off the hood of the car, and I see the girl hitchhiker bending her head against it, hunching her pack higher on her shoulders as she walks along the edge of the road.

We return through the rain, the drizzle, finally the sunshine to Kalama on the other side of the island. The campground is deserted except for a passel of hitchhikers sitting on the wall beside the road. As I park the car, the girl with the baby emerges from the ditch across the road. Inside the campground wall, only the spread–out sleeping bag, like a rug, is left of their campsite. The plastic triangle is down; the pack, gone.

I get out and go to where the girl stands talking with one of the fellows sitting on the wall.

"What happened?" I say. The back of the baby, who is held over her shoulder like a flour sack, is full of mosquito welts. She is sullen, angry, as if I were part of it too.

"They kicked everybody out," she says. The fellow with whom she has been talking hitches himself, still seated, along the wall back to his buddies.

"Who kicked everybody out?"

"The police," she says. "This morning."

"For how long?"

She shakes her head, patting the rump of the kid. "They just came and kicked everybody out." A missing lower tooth makes the face all the more ugly. "Goddamn them," she says not so much to me as to the coconut trees, the sky, the white–foamed, blue breakers beyond the campground curling toward shore.

I return to Cathy in the car. "I'd better call the county office," I say, "and find out what's going on."

She gets out of the car. "What did the girl say?"

"The police kicked everyone out this morning right after we left."

Across the road in a free–throw circle of dirt is a filling station with a phone booth, and I call the county office from there. Cathy has gone to talk with the girl.

The voice at the other end of the line is that of the younger secretary. I explain that the campground at Hana is closed, where according to her record and that of the police we are supposed to be camping that night. When I finish, it is through a giggle that she tells me that the campground at Hana has been opened again.

"I'm back at Kalama," I tell her, my voice tight. "Can we stay here tonight?"

"Just a minute," she says. I hear the snickering from the other desk before the voice, hyphenated with laughter, says, "Yes, you can."

I tell her my name.

"Change the date on your permit," she tells me, serious again, "and put my initials, A.K., next to it." Back of her, Form 202919 giggles again.

"Then Kalama is open?"

"Yes," she says and adds: "And Hana, too."

I come back to where Cathy stands with the girl beside the wall. "They've opened it up again," I tell them. The girl's eyes, as I talk, are the flat, blue–grey of a stone.

I pitch our tent in the same place as before. The fellow who is with the girl this time hauls their pack from the bushes across the road and tosses it over the wall next to the open sleeping bag. As I pound in one after the other of the tent stakes with my length of pipe, I find myself driving them as deep in the ground as they will go, burying the head around the canvas loop.

It is the middle of the night when I hear the voices, loud, insistent, near the wall, and waking up, see the headlights parked on the road. Cathy stirs beside me. "What's that?" she says.

Outside is the red flick of a police light as it comes around on the side of our tent, and I hear the girl's voice and then the baby. I fumble among my clothes at the head of the tent until I find the flashlight. "I don't know," I say. I wait, upraised on an elbow. The voices outside slide upward, garbled with anger, with shouting.

But suddenly they die away, the red flickering stops, the headlights back up and turn, the car goes down the road, leaving its noise behind like the diminishing wake of a boat. I lie back in my sleeping bag, the flashlight at my side.

Behind the scraping of the coconut fronds and the sound of the ocean breaking on the beach begins again the whine of the kid, repeating, persistent, like a tree toad in the darkness, and I don't know what to do with it yet, because my brother and Heinie and I are sitting in a wedge of sunlight in Heinie's garage waiting for Shebie's motorcycle to turn into the driveway. We have just come back from rifling Mrs. Sengstock's plum tree, except that they were green, and she has come out on the backporch, her hair in curlers, yelling at us. "I'm going to call Shebie," she shouts across her vegetable garden and her line of red hollyhocks. "You boys on Edison Street. This is the *last* time."

Penates

"*You* shouldn't swear," his daughter said from across the dinner table. "Tim doesn't."

"Watch what you say, young lady," her mother warned.

He said nothing because he couldn't think of anything to answer just then to a daughter of eighteen whose eyes looking into his were the color of his own, whose chin sometimes squared like his in obduracy as if an anvil lay just below the curve of flesh. "You mean I'm not allowed to say, 'Damned bastards,' in my own house, the windows closed, the neighbors away on vacation?"

"No," she said, "you're not. You don't want me to."

"Be careful, young lady," her mother said, as getting up she began to clear the table of the dinner plates, the salad, the basket of rolls.

"There's a difference," he reminded his daughter, "between you and me: I'm a father and you're a daughter." It was obtuse enough to sound like a father, but it had been a long, hot morning of summer–school classes.

"Tim doesn't," she repeated as if her boyfriend or whatever he was, instead of being an adolescent with a white Honda that he parked like a racer in the middle of the driveway whenever he came over, was a Paladin of infinite promise even though whenever he, himself, saw him he was wearing a surfer's sweatshirt that belonged in the laundry, and black basketball shoes as permanent as if they were the color of his feet.

"What has that Class III clerk in a grocery store got to do with my language," he said, "B.A., M.A., Ph.D.?" A smile swept like a shadow across his daughter's lips. She picked up her glass of milk and sipped, replacing it carefully on the placemat near the edge of her plate. "He doesn't swear," she said without looking at him.

"I'll make him a medal from the lid of a soup can," he offered, "and you can print on it: 'My name is Tim. I am a good boy. I do not swear.' "

"That's enough," his wife said to them both as she came back to the table.

"Then teach your daughter some manners."

"She's your daughter too, and I've told you myself you shouldn't swear. It's something that . . ." and she stopped, searching for the lady–like phrase—"doesn't become you."

"Oh my God," he said. His daughter was smiling again as if he were a small boy much younger than she who in eighteen years had learned more than he had in fifty. "Maybe if her boyfriend is so charming, you could convince him to park his scooter somewhere other than in the middle of my driveway."

"It isn't a scooter," his daughter said. "It's a Honda."

"Scooter, Honda, whatever the hell you want to call it, tell him to park the damn thing somewhere else." He inserted the *damn*, the *hell*, like bait along the sentence to see how quickly mother and daughter would react.

"You shouldn't use that kind of language," his wife said, "even if you are angry." His daughter sipped her glass of milk in mother approval, in silent support.

"Do you know why I like to play tennis?" He got up, pushing back his chair. "It saves me from having to . . ." and he left them sitting together at the table as if he were punishing them.

His wife's words followed him toward his study: "Well, you don't have to swear; you're not in the army."

He didn't have to, but it helped. He picked up from his desk the novel he was reading—a disjointed account of a comic hero who was so intelligent he could always see how funny getting his leg cut off was, and went to the patio where his porch swing like a hammock hung beneath the arching branches of the Chinese elm.

"Tim doesn't," he said, mimicking his daughter's voice. He arranged the pillows behind his head and opened the book. But the voices of mother and daughter flowed toward him from the house in an unending confluence, so that he read with something less than sympathy about a thick–nosed, sad–eyed Jew having his back scrubbed in his bath by his Japanese girl-friend, and it was only minutes later that he found himself with the open book flattened face downward across his chest while he sorted out for himself—beside the oleander's crimson blossom, next to the acacia's shadowing—the probable possibilities of the summer ahead, with a daughter in love getting ready for college and a wife who, at times, seemed to him not the girl he remembered. But beyond the afternoon's tennis, the lines entangled themselves in the chrome intricacies of a Honda's tailpipe and wrapped themselves in whimsey around the handles of his daughter's straw portmanteau—his wife, intervening, only making matters worse.

He tried to recall a gesture, a phrase, that might

have begun it all, but there was none. And it was futile in any case. What was left him now was to assess, if he could, how deep were the shelves that separated one island from another—he, his daughter, his wife. But even as he tried, he knew he had no plumb line for such measuring. He could only guess.

He closed the book, got up, and went to the house, to the ritual of his white tennis shorts, to the shoes laced across his arch, to the racket, light and responsive in his hand when he took it from its corner in his study.

He played at Los Altos Park, an enclave of six courts surrounded by greenery—by eucalyptuses, their branches thinning away into the blue; by lantana mounding against the backstops outside in a moat of small purple flowers. He walked through the gate carrying in one hand his racket, his nylon windbreaker over his arm; in the other, the Japanese carpenter's bag in which he kept the balls, his white hat, his Band-Aids, some loose change, a towel. It was his identity at the courts—the guy with the Japanese bag. The ideograms painted on its sides said something—the name and address of a Tokyo lumber company someone had told him. But enigma enough. The step into the fenced-in court was like diving into water—from heat into coolness, from mugginess into clarity, from a smile not a smile to a white line two inches wide.

Lounging on the green benches at the edge of the courts were his friends, acquaintances—something—those people he knew only by their first names, knew only by the shape of their knees below their tennis shorts, by the peculiarities of their services as they threw up the ball, by the angle of this one's cut-shot and the loop of that one's backhand drive. It had its own white vestments, its deuces and advantages and ultimate tabulations. If he sometimes lost, he also sometimes won. It seemed fair enough, and the breeze from the ocean, above the backstops, moved the bronze–green heads of the eucalyptuses in curtsies of agreement whenever he glanced their way.

Inside the gate he stopped. All the courts were filled —a geometry of white balls in flight, of crisscrossing players. But sitting on the bench across the way beside court #4 was Dante Paliano, hands thrust into his jacket pockets, wearing his tennis hat a mounded white mushroom in the distance far down over his eyes.

He skirted the playing and went toward him, plopping his bag down beside the bench and arranging his jacket over one end of the back. Dante had a desert cabin where he was fixing up a reservoir on weekends, and his son had just married an American Field Service student in Madrid, but his tennis problems were simple enough—he had a serve like a balloon.

He sat down beside him motioning with his head to where on the court before them Earl and Ron were overwhelming two members of the high–school tennis team. "Should we challenge?"

Dante sat up, taking his hands from his jacket pockets. "It's 5–1 already."

When the set was over, he opened a can of new balls, balancing them, fresh and white, on the strings of his racket as he walked onto the court to warm up with Dante. For the moment there were no daughters with boyfriends in black basketball shoes, or if there were, they were sails tinied to toys along the edge of the horizon. He sent his drives without effort off forehand and backhand, and his volleys at the net surprised even him, Dante's shots intercepted and returned to that corner, to that white line. There was a statue of Hermes in the Los Angeles museum, life–

size, leaning on a wayfarer's pedestal, a *via venturus*, the muscles firm across the abdomen, the head in its rounded cap slightly inclined, listening, amused, to the tales the dryads were telling him, and he took Dante's next shot at the net and angled it out of reach deep to the far corner more accurately than any Honda rider he knew feathering a truck on the freeway.

So that when Earl and Ron returned to the court, and Dante joined him on his side of the net, the set ready to begin, he carried with him to the baseline as he began to serve a euphoria of his own, bouncing the ball once before he tossed it skyward against the blue background and brought his racket head up to meet it. He was already halfway to the net before Earl's return arced toward him and he picked it off with a volley into the alley. For the moment there were no sun glintings off chrome–plated Honda mufflers, no surge of power as the kid twisted the throttle. He served again, and the back of Dante's white hat moved to angle away the return. The ocean eating into the shore was miles away, hidden beyond the green, attendant trees.

Later, when he turned the car into his driveway, the white Honda like a horse at a hitching post waited beside the ivy, its leather seat a modified saddle, its insignia fixed like a crusader's badge on the curved side of its gasoline tank. Inside the house, his daughter's friend slouched in the living–room armchair reading the late–afternoon paper, his black basketball shoes propped up on the footstool, his daughter's voice chattering to him from her room as she got ready to leave.

As he came through the door, the boy looked up from his paper and said, "Hi."

"Hello," he said without stopping.

"Playing tennis?"

"I think so," he answered, and he raised his racket in

a demonstration it was not a golf club. But the kid wasn't worth the silliness he evoked.

"Ah, hello," his daughter said, meeting him in the hall. "You've been pretending you're young again." It was the tone used for his tennis playing, an aberration that the family tried to keep their friends from knowing about. Long ago, he had gone to the courts with her to teach her how to hold a racket, how to step into a shot, but the ones she took in a feminine, net–facing flailing were the most accurate; while following his instructions, she sent the ball caroming against the backstop over his head or ricocheting off the net posts. He suspected, at times, she did it deliberately to show him how wrong he could be.

"Not pretending," he said. "For example, my serve today . . ."

"I bet." And finished with him, with the old man, shorts and shirt drenched with sweat, walking toward his bedroom, she turned to Tim, and her voice clothed itself in gloves and came to the edge of the upraised paper as if bearing a pillowed treasure.

His wife joined him in the bedroom where he sat on the edge of the bed tugging at the sweat–tightened knot of his tennis shoe.

"You play too long?" she said as if she could see in the curve of his back, the angle of his bent head, some fatal indication of how exhausted he was supposed to be.

"No, I didn't play too long"; he carefully removed the irritation from his voice. He eased the tennis shoe off the matted hotness of his sweat socks and tossed the shoe with a kick of his toe into the open closet where it landed end up in a corner.

"You look tired," she said.

"I am," and he bent to the other shoe, unlaced it, kicked it into the closet after the other. "I like being tired. I don't have to think then. 'Only thinking lays lads underground.' "

"Oh come," she said. After thirty years she had already measured, she implied, the depths of all his profundities and he needn't pretend cosmological and eschatological repercussions with her about the aching of his shoulder muscle or the pinched nerve of his finger.

She said it with just enough of a sigh for him not to allow it to pass: "It keeps me from thinking too long about a teen–age kid lounging in my living room every time I come home, sprawled on the couch, his feet on my coffee table as if he were doing me a favor by being here at all."

"He's nothing of the kind. He's a nice boy, and you don't have to show every time you meet him that you don't like him."

"I love him," he said. "At eighteen he knows the answers to all the problems of the world. I just don't like his feet on my coffee table."

"Don't be like that," she said, going to the dresser where she made a pretense in the mirror of fluffing up the ends of her hair.

He lay back on the bed. Don't be *like that*. It was her deflector in an argument, her favorite gambit to entrap him into trying to defend "like that," which she said in a way that gathered around the words supposedly all the barnacles of his intransigence. So he said, smiling: "But I *am* like that. I want that teen–age Marlborough man in my living room to get his basketball shoes off my coffee table."

"You're just being childish," she said as she went toward the door in what she wanted him to believe was a beldame dudgeon against his boorishness.

"And tell him to park his damn kiddycart somewhere else than in my driveway," but he was saying it to an averted face, to a hand reaching backward to close the bedroom door on the difficult member of the family.

He heard the mother–daughter whisperings in the hall, and then the voices, coated with cordiality, went to the living room, and then the outer door opened and closed, and he heard the tinkle of the bell at the street gate, the starting roar of the Honda, and he closed his eyes as the puttering, toy explosions of the cycle withdrew, tunneling out of the side street into the traffic on Palo Verde. He saw his daughter seated behind the helmet of black hair, her hands clasped from behind around the blue windbreaker, her own long hair, lifted by the wind, streaming behind in a Lochinvar, wind–riding fancying into the west; her black and white stretch–pants stirruped beneath her heels, her white blouse a surplice of simplicity through the coursing air. He followed them to the stop light at Stearns where his daughter, vaudevilling the kid, touched her toe to the ground, balancing, while they waited for the red eye to blink green. Then shoving off, they scooted, in a left–hand leaning before the oncoming traffic, onto Stearns and were gone. He got up from the bed and began to undress. Wrapping a towel around his waist, he started for the shower. At the mirror in the hall he paused a moment. Unless he held his breath, that was, he knew, no Hermes solar plexus, and the close–cropped hair was not the same stubble he had doused in the washbasin of his helmet in Italy twenty years before, so that it was at the eyes that he was forced to stop finally. *Indomitable* was the word he assigned them, and he carried it like a fresh bar of soap along with him to the shower.

Late that night, lying in bed, his wife a humped

mound of turned–away blanket beside him, he listened to the tree frogs outside the open window, hearing faintly too the traffic on Palo Verde, an elongated spindle of softened noise as a car came and went. His daughter there, among strangers, in the nighttime. He poked the mound beside him and when it stirred, he said: "When, in your mother conference, did you tell her she had to be in?"

A hand, an elbow, disentangled itself from the edge of the blanket. "What?" his wife said, turning her head toward him.

He articulated slowly: "When, in your mother's agreement, did you tell her she had to be home?"

His wife reached for the small clock on the bedside table. "What time is it?" She picked up the clock bringing it in front of her face. In the dimness of the bedroom her white arms had slendered to girlhood above the blanket.

"I don't care what time it is," he said. "I asked you when you told her to be home."

His wife turned on the reading light over the head of the bed and looked at the clock. "It isn't even twelve," she said, putting the clock back on the table. "I told her to be home at two." She turned off the light, jounced back on the bed, wrapped the blanket over her shoulder.

He lay looking out the bank of windows next to the bed, at the outlined branches of the tree there which in black, slender pencils fanned from the trunk across the grey black of the sky. A jet coming in from the ocean, its red light blinking, coasted in an even, descending line toward the airport. In the frayed edges of wind from its motors, the tree frogs were quiet. He gently touched the nosewheel to the ground between the channel of white runway lights and began rolling to a measured stop at the edge of the field.

It was only later that he awoke to the sound of the Honda coming off Palo Verde onto his street, and to the cut–off acceleration as it gutter–dipped up the incline of his driveway. And then his daughter's laughter came over the palings of the grape–stake fence, sounds like blossoms floating toward him in the darkness, followed by the guttural masculinity of the boyfriend's voice, and the Honda motor revved in a quick surge of power before it was turned off. Then silence while the tree frogs began again. Ten minutes. Fifteen. The darkness extended itself like a bolt of silk cloth unwinding, until the Honda surged again, and the noise took off down the street, the horn a jaunty beep–beep of farewell as it left, and then the tinkle of the bell on the gate and his daughter's slow footsteps returning up the walk to his door.

At breakfast the next morning her scrubbed face across the table glistened in curving petals of freshness and her hair drawn backward made her face a mask of Innocence. He searched for a Honda oil smudge on the lobe of an ear, the impression of an unfaded fingerprint on her cheek, the wavering line of a bruised lip. But there was none. She could have been just born, sea–emerging. He scooped out his grapefruit segments with slow deep jabs. Directly across from him his wife talked. What she was saying came to him like a list of names from a telephone book—long and uninterrupted and not to be listened to. It was about shopping and a topcoat for his daughter for college and a sale of pillowcases at Bullocks and . . . . He pushed his finished grapefruit aside and cracked open his soft–boiled egg. "How would you like to play tennis this afternoon?" he asked his daughter. Even though he pretended to be carefully circling free the egg from its shell with the tip of his knife, he saw her movements stop in a marble immobility across the table.

"Me?" she said as if he had mistaken her for a mermaid.

"Don't you play tennis?" He added the butter and salt to his egg—two taps with his finger on the salt shaker, a thin curling leaf of butter. He did it the same every morning—more because his wife expected him to than because he wanted to. It gave her something to fall back on in their arguments—his orderliness, his fastidiousness.

"What's the matter with Doug?" his daughter said. "Or Marie?" Marie was a joke in the family or was meant to be. It was the name his wife and daughter assigned to any of the girls he might play tennis with at the courts. And there *was* a Marie there on weekends, a forty–five year old employee of the Star–Kist tuna factory in San Pedro with whom he played doubles now and then and who had a maddeningly effective forehand drive that she hit from off her shoe tops.

"I don't want to play with Marie," he said. "I want to play with you."

She looked at her mother for help.

"We thought we would take the car and get her topcoat today," his wife said.

His daughter waited for him to answer, but when he said nothing, she added: "Tim said he might take me to the beach this afternoon. If you don't mind?"

"You could bring him along and I'll teach him too."

She looked at her mother again.

"We'll drop you off at the courts," her mother said to him, "if you really want to play."

"I want to play with her." He nodded toward his daughter. But his cause was already lost. It had been lost before he had begun.

"Some other time," she said looking directly at him. But intended as reassurance, as promise, the eyes looked at him, he saw, from across the long green reaches of a mountain meadow, her figure diminished to childhood, her face a flower on the fringe of the pine woods across the way. Between them, over the marsh grass and the lupine, the butterflies dipped in arabesques of sculptured air whose shape he struggled to hold in his mind, as if in those curves and loopings the answer were being written. But it was no use. All that remained, all that would remain, was the sun–drenched vacancy of the meadow between them, the marsh grass stiff, the butterflies slipping away, like severed kites, to wand–tip dots against the darker trees.

His daughter's face across the table came together again like a vase, still looking at him, and he said, dissembling too: "Perhaps sometime between the top-coat and the cashmere sweater."

"Cole's have some new slacks," her mother was saying, "and we can have lunch at . . . ." But neither his daughter nor he was listening.

"All right," she said to him. It was a truce, a moratorium, while he mapped out where the new lines between them might be, what final changes could be accomplished before the coming of fall and the rains, and she moved northward five–hundred miles, the daily meetings with him at an end. "Get out of my life," she had shouted at him in anger once, and, leaving, her face had burned like a brand carried toward the door of his study, and the edge of her plaid skirt had snapped like a wind–caught wave as it disappeared around the door jamb.

That was true—he would be getting out of her life. That was no longer the question. It was what image of him she would be carrying with her, like Lares, like Penates, that concerned him now. He wanted it to be accurate; he wanted it to be his—his of him, he admitted. And perhaps later, older, she would perceive it too, would understand, would understand him.

But it was only by accident that he found the way. Or thought he had. That afternoon at the tennis courts MacNeill beat him, someone who had never done it before, and seeing the smile coming toward him to the net after the last point, he saw what benefits might accrue around losing, what camaraderie might be accorded ineptitudes. After the game he sat with Mac-Neill on the bench beside the court while opening up to him were family anecdotes never uncovered before, as if he had, by losing, become a close relative whose opinions, MacNeill found, fit his own like the mortising of a dresser drawer in a happy, sliding smoothness.

Finally he broke away, wrapped the towel around his neck, zipped his racket head into its protective cover, and, the friend of everyone, fled homeward in his Volkswagen. Was that the way? To lose? And by losing win?

When he pulled the Volkswagen into the driveway, the white Honda stood on its kickstand in front of the garage door. In a last assertion of something or other, he stopped the green curve of the VW fender a few inches from the Honda's front wheel—a confrontation that his daughter need not see, to show one last time the accuracy with which he could put his serve into either corner. And when he came around the front of the car, he saw that the chrome bumper nudged the corrugated rubber pedal of the Honda in a finite measuring of old–man accomplishment. He left it there, a vanguard flag plunged into the sand for the enemy to find.

In the living room, as he came through his study on his way to the bedroom, his daughter's boyfriend was hunched in the armchair near the window reading a magazine. From his daughter's room down the hall came the contrapuntal playing of mother and daughter voice, the chitchat of viola answering violin in a chamber–music dialogue for a quiet afternoon. It was their answer to his tennis, he knew—exemplum.

"Hello," he said to the back cover of the magazine held before the boy's face. He did not stop for an answer but continued toward his room. Beside his going, he saw the abrupt lowering of the magazine, heard the "Oh, hello," as if he were an interruption to serenity, as he supposed he was—the father, the other male. He smiled at the image in the hallway mirror as he passed—*tyrannus rex*—with a kneecap that buckled at odd moments, a shoulder that cortisone had long ago failed to cure, a wrist that to play tennis needed a layered band of supporting tape that when he took it off after the game left a white bracelet of untanned skin like a manacle to infirmity.

The door to his daughter's room opened as he went past, and his wife's voice followed him along the hall and into his bedroom: "I thought that was you." The figure followed the voice, a fish at the end of a line.

He tossed his bag with his tennis equipment into the corner near the dresser, leaned his racket against the wall, came over and sat on the bed to take off his shoes. She came and sat beside him, carrying carefully like a full glass of water whatever she was gong to say. Even sitting there as mother emissary, he liked her. He had always admitted it, and he realized in a lurch of affection how accurate had been the high school attraction of how many years ago? thirty? thirty–five? that instead of diminishing had become for him instead a series of disclosures as imperceptible as the shifting of the world's axis, as if each week, each day, the sun had uncovered for a moment the colored striations along a canyon wall he had never noticed before. She was that to him—familiar and unfamiliar—

even to the shape of her breasts, the inflection of a phrase, the toeing of sand in front of her as they had walked along the beach the previous night, the lights along Belmont Pier marching like a column of soldiers off the tip of blackness into the ocean, but they, she, no longer the same, that day gone.

She was that changing pleasure to him, he had always admitted. But sometimes when not only time but landscape altered as well, he found himself clambering from despair, because all that remained unfaded of the four days of camping with her below Ensenada last month was the image of a kid squatting near an irrigation ditch, his underpants, from behind, almost touching the ground, his hand shoving up an island of mud in the water as their car passed. She too, at the car window seeing, no longer then the same with him as before the not seeing. So that yoked to his happiness with her there was also the knowledge that out of the pleasures that living with her meant, only a few would he manage to fix, like a photograph, would he be able, finally, to keep.

So that as she sat beside him on the bed and he bent to untie his shoes, he channeled his attention in a locked waveband to her voice, to the hands in her lap, to see what an afternoon's mutation had wrought.

"Now what?" he said. He made his voice into that of a loser, from the other side of a moat.

"What's the matter? Someone beat you?"

"If someone beat me, it's only because I let him," he told her.

"I suppose that's right," she admitted, and she paused to examine the fact a moment before filing it away—something that she had known but only now realized. "I suppose that's right."

"Not really," he said. "He was luckier than usual." He kept on undressing while they talked—shoes, socks, getting up and stripping off his white sport shirt over his head.

"Mary wants to know whether she and Tim can go to the Cave tonight."

He told himself later that at least they could have let him shower first. "What the hell is the Cave?" he said, his voice, in spite of himself, honed to asperity.

"It's a coffeehouse on 101 near Laguna Beach."

He said nothing. He got up and went to the closet for a fresh towel. "Tell Mary I want to see her," he said finally, his role of loser already spilling over into anger. His wife got up from the edge of the bed, and he heard their voices in the other bedroom and then his wife returned like a bridesmaid in a retinue and sat once again on the edge of the bed and his daughter behind her came and stood in the doorway leaning against the door jamb. She was wearing an orange, shift–like dress with brown seed beads looped two or three times around her neck, her blonde hair pulled backward behind her ears. Bare feet in the slimness of sandal straps, she had stopped somewhere in an Egyptian courtyard; bronzed, she leaned somewhere against a fluted pillar.

"Now what is this all about?" he said.

"What is what all about?" She stayed, leaning against the door jamb, conceding nothing, admitting nothing.

"I told you," her mother said to him from the bed: "she and Tim want to go to the Cave tonight. Can they or can't they?"

"On that cycle–rammer of his? On Highway 101?"

"You *could* let us have the car," his daughter said, "if you don't want me on the Honda." It was the either–or blackmailing that hardened him the most.

"There's another alternative," he said; "you neither go on the Honda nor take the car. You stay home." He said it like an ultimatum. She raised an eyebrow, pushed herself away from the door jamb with her shoulder, and turned to leave.

"Wait," her mother said, and turned to him. "We're not using the car tonight, are we?" as if she couldn't understand what he was objecting to.

"So?"

"They're only going to the Cave."

"That's all right, Mother," his daughter said as she turned and walked down the hall toward her room. The voice carried with it a commiserating weariness. "Don't argue with him."

His wife got up. "You're just being unreasonable," she told him, and she too left.

He undressed the rest of the way, draped a towel around his waist and went to the shower. Where was the father image of himself he had planned, bowing out before the curtain closed, a faint smile on his lips? He dropped the towel as a bathmat outside the shower stall, and reaching in turned on the water, adjusted it. He stepped into the shower and slid the door shut behind him, ducking his head beneath the spray in a closed–eye, breath–holding anger—at them, at himself.

That night at the dinner table, he said to the silence arranged against him—to his daughter's hands held in her lap, to the head across the table tilted in submission to the circle of soup as if it were a monstrance before which she bowed: "All right, go. Who can stand the martyred look of adolescents who think they are being abused. Go out with that Tom Mix to the Cave or wherever the hell you want to go." Was that what he had intended to say? that the image? His daughter's soup spoon stopped at the edge of her plate.

"You needn't swear," she said, and the tone of

reprimand was that of her mother. "If you don't want us to go, we won't go, that's all."

"We won't go . . ." he mimicked.

"Now stop," her mother said.

He put down his own soup spoon and talked to them both over the tepee of his hands. "I want her to go. There's a nice abutment over the Marina on 101 with just enough curve at the top so that a skidding Honda at fifty–five or sixty could take off the front two or three feet of concrete without any trouble at all."

His daughter looked at him unabashed as if he were a deep–sea specimen behind an aquarium glass—fearsome but harmless. She bent her head once more to the soup, a smile like a wind's passing moving across her face. "We haven't hit it yet," she said.

"That's enough," her mother said, so that he turned to her then, diverted, as both his daughter and wife knew he would be.

"Enough what? Enough of her?"

"Enough of you both," his wife said. "You said she could go; let her go."

His daughter, eyes down, continued with her soup.

It wasn't the way he had intended it to happen, the way he had hoped, but he let her pass him then like a landmark that she had used until now but no longer needed. In the distance was a white Honda with a seated figure waiting in its saddle, a foot touching the ground, poised for flight. He wished in a last regret that it might have been some other figure, but it was not. And in fact he had no way of assessing what that black helmet of hair might become. It was enough for her that it was not a thick–waisted tennis player. And she was right, but for him it didn't make her going any easier.

"He'd better be careful, that's all," he said so that she could see what daily obsolescence accumulated in fathers. She looked up and smiled. Understanding? Sympathy? He would never know.

"Somebody *did* beat you at tennis," she said.

"All the time," he answered. "Every day."

So that after dinner when Tim came to pick her up, he himself was on the swing on the patio, the green bulge of the pittosporum branches hiding him from the door of the house. All he could see after the noise of the Honda had stopped outside in the driveway were the black basketball shoes and legs coming up the sidewalk, stopping in front of the door. And then his wife's voice invited the legs in, and the screendoor opened, and he was alone on the patio again in the semidarkness, the greens of the garden fading to grey, to black; the three clay bells at the other end of the yard, suspended on a single thong from his olive tree, only wedges of shadow one above the other. The breeze from the ocean had gone, and the leaves waited immobile. And he too. Until below the pittosporum branches the bottom of the door swung open again and the black basketball shoes stepped out followed by the leather sandals of his daughter, her tanned legs. "Good-night, Mother," she said; "we'll be home by two." The screen door shut, and he watched the basketball shoes walk toward the gate at the far end of the garden, watched the sandals follow them, disappearing. He heard the tinkle of the gate opening and closing, and listened while he envisioned the boy swinging his leg over the saddle of the Honda, saw his daughter get on behind him, propping her straw purse in her lap between them. Then the motor sputtered and was gunned, and in his mind he followed them as they glided down the driveway in the twilight, turned onto the street. At the Palo Verde stop sign they paused a moment, but then tilting together, joined the traffic on Palo Verde and were gone .

He came back within the grape–stake fence, back along the black pool of his lawn, along the flagstones before the patio—back within the coffin silence of the swing. Without thinking, he watched the darkness fill up the yard, obliterating leaves into masses of shadow, drowning the blossoms of the oleander, diminishing the sidewalk to a pencil of grey leading to the gate. His own hand in the darkness showed only the white gleam of its fingernails, and then after a while, when he glanced down, that whiteness too had disappeared, and he was suspended alone in the darkness hearing the amaryllises along the fence inching upward in the night.

The Piranha

My older brother, Frank, married one of the most unattractive girls I have ever seen, and I liked her immediately. When I first saw them together after they were married—my brother, wide-shouldered, stocky, morosely staring at the sidewalk; she, thin, with hair that curled and twisted and drooped like a sick vine from a flower pot—my heart leaped up.

"Ah," I said, "you married her," as if I could see all the jouncing and turning he had done on his cot in the YMCA making up his mind about her since I had seen him with her that first time, a clerk in the dime store.

A smile, apologetic and abasing, came to her lips and faded, like an uncertain ripple sinking back into the water.

I was working on the west coast and had come back to my mother's home in northern Wisconsin during my vacation. It was a blackmail of affection that I resented but agreed to. Cathy had gone on to New York to some friends. "You your way; I, mine," she had said, lightly, patronizing, while we waited for her train to leave Chicago. And coming north then that night through the towns along the lake, the old baggagemen at the stations taking their time against the roses on the tables of the diner, I half regretted not going with her. Until I met my brother with his wife in Green Bay. It compensated for the two listless weeks I was to waste in the little town where my mother still lived.

Sitting on the swing on the front porch, as I used to, with its green–striped, faded canvas pad and its black velvet cushions, I worked out then the circuitous journeying that had brought Frank to where I had found him.

As boys we had quarreled incessantly—about baseball mitts, about skates, even about marbles. "What do you want *those* for?" I remember taunting him as we sat on the figured carpet of the living room. The pile of special marbles he had cupped in front of him were red with whorls of white twisting through and around and into the density of the center. They were like the calf's heart that a farm boy had brought to biology class, with its arteries, its streaks of fat, disappearing mysteriously into the red pulp of silenced thumping.

The ones in front of me were flawlessly clear with not even small bubbles to interrupt their glimmering when they were held up to the light. "What do you want *those* for?" he countered, and neither of us knowing the answer then rolled the marbles in front of us closer together, while the sun lay like a net over both of us.

So that when he went to join the CCC's after high school, the Depression already begun, I watched impassively in the dining room while he put down his checkered sport jacket on the crocheted tablecloth in order to kiss my mother goodbye. He was to be stationed near Eagle River and was to be kept busy planting pine trees along the mountain slopes of the cut–over timber land. I shook his hand, I think, but still held a finger in the book I was reading and, after he had gone, while my mother was wiping the tears from her cheeks with the back of her hand, returned to the swing on the front porch to resume among the cushions the story that his leaving had interrupted.

He came back sporadically during the years I was in high school, unannounced, his cheeks permanently brownish–red from the weather, his hands stubbier, his shoulders wider. Sitting under the lamps at night, my mother sewing, I reading, we would hear the sudden bound of his boots on the front porch, the br—rr—rr of the doorbell, the rattle of the doorknob. It was a ritual he followed and enjoyed each time he came home. The net curtain across the oval window of the door would flatten itself as the door was shoved open, and my brother would be there—in a hurry because the fellows were waiting in the car outside—dumping small leather purses on the dining room tablecloth, that he had made at night somewhere up north there, turning on the light in the kitchen to see the stove, the square, white kitchen table against the wall, and, satisfied, coming back to the room where I still sat, my book open on my knees.

Meanwhile my mother, after kissing him, would have gone hastily into the bedroom off the dining room, where she slept, and which was separated by curtains from the other room, would have lifted up the rug under the far corner, and would have taken out from under the brass leg of the bed the money hidden there, so that when my brother came back into the living room, she would be standing there with a dollar bill rolled up tightly in her hand that she would slip into his jacket pocket.

"Be good, Frank," she would say as if he were lost in a wilderness, not of underbrush but of wickedness, that our lack of money had driven him to.

He would kiss her, embarrassed, while she framed his face with her hands, and tell her, "Don't worry, Mother. I'll be all right."

How much he resented going back into the darkness beyond the door, I don't know, but while he talked, he looked to see what had been moved in the house, what remained, of those familiar objects that already to me were becoming slightly ridiculous—the cake in the form of a life–sized lamb, coconut covered, that my mother preserved in the china closet among her hand–painted plates and her gold–trimmed cream and sugar pieces, the pendulum clock on the dish–railing near the staircase, the red, tesselated lamp shade on the library table. Once reassured by them, he became almost jovial.

"And how are you?" he would say, turning to me, as if I too were a precious object from which he was holding back the cold, infringing nights of those northern woods.

"All right," I told him, so that finding nothing more to say, he would leave again for five or six months and wouldn't bother me, while my mother for a few weeks would make me stop reading on the porch swing and drive me out to the garage and the lawn mower even though the grass wasn't worth mowing. But later she would forget the impact of my brother's standing near the dining room table smelling of crushed bark, and I would be allowed to go back to my porch swing and the book kept under the pillow.

When I finished high school three years later, the worst of the Depression was over, and there was some hope of my going to college. All during the summer there were explosive conversations between my mother and father on the broken–down glider on the back porch, my father's voice getting louder and louder until even I, reading on the swing in front, could hear it: "I don't care what the neighbors think. *You* going to send him?" And my mother for a few days would wash the dishes with restrained violence as she thought up new arguments against him for me.

It was my brother, however, his three years in

the CCC's finished, who finally decided it. He came home the summer after my graduation, much older, it seemed, much quieter, as if the mere number of pine trees, counted up, that he had planted each year and now growing in the woods disheartened him, and I, looking up from my book on the porch swing, noticed for the first time, when he climbed out of the car pulled up at the curb, the rigid creases in the heavy boots he wore and the listlessness with which the knapsack dangled from his shoulder. It was as if he had exhausted forever the color of the jack–in–the–pulpits, the arbutuses, the smell of the tarpaper shacks they lived in and had come home now to recuperate.

His coming stopped for a while my mother's arguments with my father, for even she saw, I presume, the disparity between us then, and she avoided for weeks talking to my father about me, because going through the house restlessly but carefully, as if he were in a gingerbread cottage that he had grown too big for, was the uneasy, homeless figure of my brother.

He was almost tempted, I think, to sign up for another three years, and to go once again into that northern wasteland to the predictable affection of woodticks and the clamoring of squirrels. My mother during the first week of his being home showered him with molasses cookies, lemon pie, and even in regretted enthusiasm (because it meant a whole day's work) a breadboard full of *kolaches*, in one sweeping payment rewarding him for all the meals of hash, stew, and beans he had eaten out of his messkit sitting on tree stumps beside some country road. But then she began to brush him out of the way from room to room while she cleaned, and when he sat down on the back steps with my father at night after supper, while the mosquitoes came humming up from the grass beside the edge of the porch, the puffs of smoke from my father's pipe were interrupted only by cautious questions about how much money he had managed to save. It wasn't much, we all knew, but my father would have liked to know how much and even I, after a while, when August was almost past and what I was to do in the fall, if anything, had not been agreed on, thought of that money he had earned from the government scraping the red clay from their shovels, clearing off the weeds from along the roads, making fire lanes through the land in the northern part of the state that not even the settlers from Kentucky or the Indians cared to live on.

A few times when my mother, a towel around her head and a broom in her hand, had shooed him out of his room upstairs because she had work to do, he had wandered out to where I was reading on the front porch and had sat down with restraint on the edge of the swing as if he were in a doctor's office uneasily trying to minimize, as he waited, his shoulders, the awkwardness of his hands.

Reluctantly, I stopped reading when he came. I had that summer been going through a collection of "Little Russian Masterpieces," and my head was full of Sashas and Fyodors and long stretches of snow and candles being lit in windows and students quarreling over cards at Petersburg.

He wanted to know what I was reading and motioned vaguely toward the book. "Pushkin," I said, a new name I had just learned that morning but which, because of the healthy cheek beside and above me, I said now as if everyone knew who he was.

"He's a Russian. A short–story writer," I explained.

"Good?" Frank asked, but he really didn't care for he was studying the cracks in the grey boards of the porch as if we had been talking about them.

I shrugged. At that time I had learned that just

being silent ballooned among the neighbors and my mother's sisters my reputation for being different, so that in their minds I was distinct from other people just because I said nothing and was found, whenever they came to call, on the swing eating crackers, a book in my hand. It was the reason, I believe, my mother thought I should go to college—an indefinite place in her mind where people read thick books and knew all the answers to innumerable questions. And ate crackers.

My brother merely nodded at my shrug. He had always as a boy made better boats from the slats of wooden lard pails, better bamboo arrows for our bows, better propellors out of balsa wood. It was my way of paying him back, I suppose, this pretended profundity, for all the infuriating cracks my fumbling had made in the sides of my boats where the nails had split the wood.

"You like to do that," he said; "read, I mean?" He spoke seriously as if marking down my answers in his mind for future significant tabulation.

"Of course," I said, because one doesn't read all day and then say he doesn't like to, although it was enough on those long summer afternoons to feel the swing arcing like a cradle beneath me, the book open on my knees but unlooked at until someone came along the sidewalk in back of me—Dr. Kesley, Bud Beatty, Mrs. Sengstock—the ones who were usually going to and from downtown. I must have been an indigestible lump even to them in their eight–to–five jobs, unless they thought of me in a limited way as being the boy on their street who would finally make good, off somewhere, beyond Milwaukee, and so tolerated me.

He got up as if having gathered all his notes he was going to his office now, like a lawyer, to make up the brief, and went upstairs to his room. I opened my book again to where Aniutka has just got in the sleigh and is saying goodbye to Vanya, and the snow fell steadily over the red peony bushes beside me and the wind driving across the dark steppes whipped little eddies of it across the porch under the swing, chilling my feet.

The next morning while I was still trying to decide from the table of contents what new story to start, Frank came downstairs and, coming out to the porch again, sat down beside me. Without preliminaries he said: "You want to go away to school?" It was the closest he had ever come to showing what I meant to him. He was rubbing the knuckles in his lap without looking at me.

I put my book down and said, "Sure. Don't you?"

He shrugged.

"You want to stay around *this* place?" and I made a motion with my head to the house with its two bay windows staring like square, jack–o–lantern eyes at the street, to the flower boxes full of geraniums that sat along the railing of the porch. "Even the CCC's is better than this place," I told him, as if I knew all about the compensations of swinging grubhoes, of catching pickaxes in the roots of a stump, of pitching a shovelful of wet clay over the sideboard of a truck.

But he wouldn't answer. "How much do you think it would cost," he went on; "to start with, I mean?"

I wondered where he had his money, in what repeated foldings it must be to fit into all the coin purses he had brought home for us, and suddenly with college now building its turrets, its sidewalks curving across sun–shrouded lawns in front of me, I said cautiously: "I don't know."

And he said, angry: "A hundred? Two hundred?"

It is a wonder, when I come to think of it, that he didn't dump me out of the swing then as he so easily could have done, and I admit, as I half expected him to do, the books and crackers on top of me.

"A hundred maybe," I said. Money to me, even during the Depression, was a worry for my parents, not for me, and when I wanted to go to the show, my father's stubby hand with its leathery skin and blue veins never failed to burrow into his side pocket and come up with a quarter, a dime, some pennies mixed with his keys. "That's all," he would say threateningly as he gave me the quarter. But he always gave it to me.

"I've got a hundred, a hundred and fifty," my brother said. I don't know whether he wanted me to ask for it or not, because he was again rubbing his knuckles as if remembering what trees they had cut down, what thick mittens they had pulled over numb hands, what blankets at night they had clamped down over his shoulders and around his ears. But it was too good a chance to lose.

"*You* going to school?" I said as if the whole idea of those stiff boots and thick pants entering the hush of a library were preposterous.

He listened with only a vague smile showing at the corners of his mouth and then, putting his two hands on his knees, got up abruptly. "No," he said. "You. You can have it if you want it," and he went back into the house without waiting for my answer. The varnished screen door with its row of spindles across the center flopped shut behind him.

I saw myself already getting off the train amidst students in sport sweaters and scuffed, expensive shoes, amidst girls with Tanya–white skin and husky voices, the purple around their eyes leading to inexplicable profundities and world epiphanies. And I went that fall to join them, my brother's money, like a sprig of moly, borne with me.

I learned from my mother some time around

Thanksgiving when she sent me a box of molasses cookies because she thought I would be homesick, that Frank had taken a job in a dental laboratory for twelve dollars a week. It seemed fair enough.

I came home those summers each year a little more dissatisfied with the boards on the back porch that were beginning to rot, with the lumps in the mattress on my bed upstairs. Now and then I stopped off to see Frank at the YMCA in Green Bay on my way back in September. He had been sending me five dollars on and off, and it seemed the least I could do. His room on the fourth floor had a single bed, a dresser with a glass top, and a window that looked out on a laundry whose jets of steam made you think of the vats of soggy, matted clothes below.

We usually, while we waited for my train at night, wound up at a bar where Frank had only to say hello to the bartender before he had his drink in front of him.

"How's Lil?" my brother would say, and the bartender, wiping his hands on his apron, would say, "Fine, fine," as if Lil never changed, and he would nod to me sitting on the stool with my white sport sweater on, its golden *C* for being on the tennis team embarrassingly large and ornamental beside his apron: "Your kid brother?"

And Frank would nod, looking into the circle of his drink and say, "Yes, this is Bill," as if I were a piece of preciousness even then that my mother kept in the utmost corner of her china cupboard and took out only for weddings, anniversaries, or deaths. "He goes to school," my brother said, as if that explained and forgave, in a way, my pared fingernails, my evenly tanned hands, my white shirt.

The bartender wiped his hands on his apron again and offered my brother a drink, on the house, he said, as if in commiseration. He forgot me entirely as if I were a child brought in to see what a bar looked like.

"He's a good guy," Frank said when we were outside again, but he let it go at that.

He waited up until the 11:20 train to see me off, and I left him there under the shed–like platform waving his hand to me uncertainly, as if he didn't see where I was, until a baggage truck lumbered in front of him and drove him back to the side of the station against the blackened bricks of the wall.

Later when I had come to borrow his car for a weekend, he introduced me to Lil for the first time. She was so unattractive at first glance that I half suspected he was very crudely making fun of the Kappa I had just pinned.

"This is Lil," he said. We were in the dime store across from the bar, and the girl was behind the cosmetic counter. I saw her over the ten–cent celluloid combs, the tiers of nail polish, the cards of hair nets and pictures of girls applying deodorant under their upraised arms in perpetual allures of feminine freshness. She smiled, a little frightened at meeting "Frank's brother," while I stood diffidently back as they made, in one–word exchanges, an agreement to meet at the bar after I had left that night.

The odor of rancid oil from the roasted–peanut case followed us out the double swinging doors, while Lil's face, I saw in the mirror beside the door, watched us, tight and apprehensive, from between the clutter of glass shelves near her cash register. We walked in silence half way back to the Y before he said anything. "She's a good kid," he said as if he were not only apologizing but also explaining something I would not understand.

Three years later, after I myself was married, he was too. He probably wouldn't have married her if it hadn't been for me, if it hadn't been for the desperation I engendered in him when I came to see him, a book in my hand, the sights of college secretively harbored from him. Perhaps the daily baseball scores chalked up in monotony on the wall of his barroom helped too. I am trying to be fair. The fish he finally bought, however, the aquariums he had in his apartment in Reseda later, I had nothing to do with.

I was on the coast and couldn't go to the wedding, but mother wrote that she was a nice girl. I sent them a telegram: "Say hello to that good guy the bartender for me," and went back to my books. That summer, at my mother's insistence, I had come home, stopping at Green Bay to see them together—married—and then, when the two weeks were over, I met Cathy in Chicago again and we went back to the coast together.

I had just finished reviewing a novel for the Sunday newspaper and had thrown the book back on the desk and the notes into the wastebasket, when Frank called. He was in a little town, Reseda, north of Los Angeles. A new job. I thought he was laughing as he talked, or perhaps slightly drunk.

"Fine," I said when he told me where he was. "The four of us can get together now."

He laughed openly then, the laughter not just a flavor around his words: "I've left her," he said.

I had a difficult time remembering her name although the disembodied face caught in the glass racks of the dime store like a battered Christmas ornament took shape graphically and instantly on the beige wall above the phone. "Lil?" I said.

"Lil," he repeated, but even as he said it, the hurt gathered around the name like the discoloration around a scar.

"What for?" I said as if he had disobeyed an order I had given. I waited for him to answer, growing impatient when I thought for a minute he had left the phone.

"She wasn't a Kappa," he said finally.

"Don't be silly."

"I'm not," he answered. "She wasn't."

"We'll come see you," I said as if the boat I had made was springing its leaks, as I expected, and foundering in my mother's washtub, the water seeping into the cracks where the nails had been driven, and the whole afternoon, waterlogged, sinking toward the galvanized, concentric ridges at the bottom of that inland sea.

"Yes," he said. "Why don't you? I've got fish now. Tropical ones." He waited for me to say something, but I let him talk. "In tanks," he went on.

"All right," I interrupted. "We'll come see your fish."

He gave us his address and telephone number.

It was two months later before we found time to take the freeway north and, after a few blocks searching in the town, pulled up in front of the apartment building in which he lived.

I had asked Cathy, joking, to wear her Kappa pin, and it hung, inconspicuous but provocative on her sweater. "For my brother," I explained. "He likes Kappa girls."

He had a drink in his hand when he opened the door and had been watching TV. The bluish–white picture going on behind him was of a bowler, with a name on his shirt, competently knocking down all of the pins in the alley. The sound of the pins' scattering came from the set around him and up to the screen door.

He was exuberant and jovial, and I could tell then, that he was drunk. "Ah, my brother," he said as he put his hand on my shoulder. "And this is Bill's lovely wife." He put the words in quotations as if he were repeating a phrase from one of my mother's letters, and briefly I was sorry for the key on Cathy's sweater, for it wouldn't have been necessary at all.

The blinds were drawn and the apartment smelled faintly of crushed cigarettes, of gin.

"Come in, come in," he said as he backed up. He went to the windows, pulling up the blinds as we came through the door, and clicked off the set where the bowler, wiping his hands on a towel, waited impatiently for his cannonball to come rolling back toward him. The picture contracted into a long alley of blackness toward a tiny moon and then that too went out.

He set his glass down near the window on the commode that my mother had apparently given him. A rocker with a needlepoint back that had been in our living room at home and two of my mother's oak–framed pictures were also in the room, and I think he had done it deliberately, just for my sake, for no one would have moved that furniture over mountains, across deserts of sagebrush, just to transform a room in an apartment building two thousand miles away into my mother's house.

"You came to see my fish," he said seriously as if he were laying out the bounds of the afternoon. He sat down in the rocker across the room.

We both sat on the couch opposite him. "You," I said, a problem we had set our minds to. But he ignored my answer.

"Wait until you see my Rose Tetra," he said, and he got up abruptly, starting toward the back of the apartment to show us the way. He turned, however, half way out, as if he had forgotten something, and came back toward Cathy. "You'd like a drink?" he said.

As he stood before her waiting for an answer, he glanced once at the key on her sweater, and Cathy, noticing, blushed. "Yes," she said too quickly; "I would."

While he mixed the drinks in the kitchen, he talked of the fish he had bought. The words came in snatches between the thud of the refrigerator door, the squeak of a cork, the clatter of a spoon thrown into the sink. He came back, a drink carefully carried in each hand, gave them to us, and sat down, so that we could only stare morosely at the olive as we sipped our drinks and he went on talking of his Blue Acaras, his Pearl Gouramis, his *Chilodus Punctatus*. He used the names purposefully, I thought, with the same offhand familiarity I had used, I remembered, when I told him at the bar one night in Green Bay that I was marrying a Kappa Kappa Gamma.

"Come see them," he said, and he waved inclusively to the rest of the apartment. He got up and we followed. He had tanks set up on window ledges, on the tops of dressers, on low tables—in the kitchen, in the two bedrooms, even in the bathroom. As we went from room to darkened room, he snapped on the lights in the aquariums and the tanks materialized dramatically all at once out of the darkness in front of us, the fish weaving their flashing patterns of color before us. "Ooh," Cathy said, at the first one, from the doorway to the den. The faint hissing sounds that had come from the darkness when we entered were the aerating bubbles flowing upward in the tanks. He showed us how the mechanism worked—by a tiny cut–off switch in back of the banks from which three rubber tubes, the size of pencils, curled and ran to their complicated duties.

He worked the switch, turning it on and off, and responsively the bubbles stopped, resumed, stopped, in the silent moving world inside the tanks.

"You should get yourself an aquarium," he said to me, smiling, but I said nothing. I rubbed my hand over Cathy's back as, bent over, she intently watched the fish glittering in front of her.

The largest tank was in his bedroom, at the foot of the bed on a low chest. It extended the full width of the bed. He had been saving it for the last. He went to the table near the head of the bed and turned on a switch. The aquarium glowed, and the fish, delicately finned, in hues of purple, orange, silver, blue, gold, drifted indolently and intricately through the water.

"I work it from here at night," he explained. He picked up the small switchboard from the end table to show us and then put it back. "It saves getting up once I'm in bed."

The aquarium had been put together like a Japanese garden, and the fish, as I watched, found themselves easing through strategically arranged plants growing in a corner, or coasting through the crevices of sunken houses, or nosing along the pavements of brilliantly colored stones.

He came around to the foot of the bed to where Cathy and I were standing. She was bending over again admiring the fish.

"That's a Scalare," he said to her as he, too, bent over and pointed to a pale white fish, with a tail fin like a scimitar, that had come to their side of the tank and was nosing upward along the glass for food, and when Cathy pointed to the brilliance of a purple–tail she had caught sight of, he said modestly: "From Siam. Fighting fish."

"Where's Lil?" I said from my place in the gloom back of Cathy, whose face was almost touching the glass side now as she peered at the weavings, the noiseless, glittering family of fish within.

But my brother pretended not to hear as bent over, his hands on his knees, he was talking to Cathy. One third of the tank was divided by a thin glass plate, which I hadn't noticed before, and a solitary fish swam there back and forth that Cathy was now watching. "That's a Piranha," he said to her. "Carnivorous." They watched together as the unblinking eyes stared back at them through the glass and the mouth opened and shut, showing the serrated teeth in two semicircle rows like a toy bear trap made of pearl. "Like razors," he said.

A black snail, sliding upward across the glass, had come to the surface, and Frank poked it down again.

Cathy stood up and half turned toward me. "Aren't they wonderful?"

"How much they cost?" I asked Frank.

"Not much," he said.

"Two hundred? Three hundred?"

"Something like that."

"Where's Lil?" I said.

He went to the head of the bed and turned off the light so that the aquarium sank back into the darkness at the foot of the bed, and all three of us had to go back to the living room.

We finished our drinks and got up to leave, but even so Frank sat in my mother's rocker across the room turning his martini glass around in his hands as if we were no longer there.

Only when Cathy began to thank him for showing

us the fish, did he get up and putting his drink down, come with us toward the door. "I've got a book . . ." He spoke to Cathy, offering, and made a suggested motion to one side of the room to get it, if she wanted, but she interrupted him.

"No thanks," she said sincerely, "but we'll come again. I promise."

I hesitated at the door while Cathy went alone down the sidewalk toward the car. "Where's Lil?" I asked him, but he shut the screen in my face.

"I fed her to the Piranha," he said.

"She was a good kid," I admonished him, and it would have been enough, I suppose, to have left him then, but I couldn't refrain from a last feinted kick at the whorled marbles gathered before him on the carpet in the living room. "But you'll have time to go to school now," as if it were something that, being my brother, he should have done long ago.

And though I waited, smiling, he wouldn't answer; so that, turning, I left him there, his face like a ghost's in the doorway while behind him in the house swam his Spotted Danios and his Rasboras and his red Helleris.

I slammed the car door on my side and pressed the starter. Cathy sat stonily in the other seat. "What did he ever do to you?"

"Nothing," I said. "I love him dearly."

She sat staring out the blue–tinted window at the flat, anonymous door of my brother's apartment. "You're a bastard," she said slowly. She measured out each of the words.

I pulled away from the curb into traffic. "Me?" half denial, half question.

"You," she said.

And to that Kappa pronouncement I could only smile, for what did that silk–sheathed, glimmering stranger, whom Lil and my mother would have cowered before, know about woodticks and brothers and porch swings and leaking boats and a coconut–covered Lamb of God who with raisin eyes stared in compassion whenever I entered the room.

Akroterion

When they drove into Athens, around the firehouse spraying of the Omonia Square fountain and slid off onto one of the side streets as if some centrifugal force had given way and they had spun out of orbit, he was already certain that the guy at the Corinth canal had shortchanged him a couple of drachma on the souvlakia they had eaten at the tables outside the tourist shop. ΕΛΛΑΣ. He couldn't even read the goddamned signs with the V's tipped upside down and the M's propped up on their sides and the L's mirrored backward. His wife Cathy in the seat beside him was turning the map of Athens around in her lap like a compass, lining up the directions of the streets.

They were caught at a stop light in four lanes of one-way traffic on some diagonal street or other. "You any idea where we are?"

"We should be right about here," she said, her finger on the map, "on Stadiou and there should be a tourist parking lot . . . ." She looked up from her map. "There!" She pointed out the window over the intervening three lanes of traffic to where a hundred or so cars were jammed in three lines before a small park. "There it is. It's right there."

The light changed and he drove where he had to, straight ahead in his own lane. "We'll go around the block," he said. But before he knew it, they had burst onto the sunlight whirligig of Syntagma Square, past some people at tables having their afternoon coffee, and out the other side—on his way to the airport, the signs said.

He stopped at the curb below one of the blue signs with a jet like a seagull flying across it. Cathy centered the map on her knees. "We've got to turn around," she said.

"Those bastards." She was used to his language now. It just meant his world had flattened out temporarily, was teetering on the backs of turtles. She looked out the car window to where a lamb tethered by one hoof outside a butcher shop was bleating in the doorway before he got slaughtered like the others for Easter. She thought he had meant the shop owners.

"Them?"

"No, not them; the people who think that everyone wants to go to the airport." But in his mind he began to list them all—the waiter in the Patras restaurant the night before who after tabulating their bill suddenly discovered he needed another eighty drachma, the attendant on the ferryboat who had him park the car so tight against the bulkhead he had to crawl over the gearshift to get out the other side. There was a whole list of them, from one end of the poppy–covered, pothole–roaded country to the other.

"We've got to turn around and go back to Syntagma Square," Cathy said, "and down Mitropoleos Street. See here." She pointed to the map. "The arrow goes in that direction, where we want to go, and there's another tourist parking place next to the cathedral."

"The bishop'll be there with his alms boxes, what do you want to bet?" He shifted into first, and when, in the rear–view mirror the stop light two blocks behind them turned red, holding up traffic, he made a U–turn back toward town. When they came again to Syntagma Square, he could hardly believe there was a left lane in the traffic for a turn onto Mitropoleos.

"You see," Cathy said as they slid past the buses parked before each of the airline waiting rooms on that side of the Square. "It's just like on the map." And it was, by some fluke of orderliness remembered from Aristotle. In two or three blocks on Mitropoleos back of the cathedral there were parking places reserved for tourists in a small square, and across the street, as if by courtesy of the travel bureau were two of the hotels listed in their *Guide to Greece*. He eased the car between a Mini–Minor with a GB tag on it and a Mercedes with a Connecticut license, feeling at home for the first time since driving off the ferry.

He sat beside Cathy in the car while she read the recommendations in the guidebook: Bright indoor cafe and lovely mirrored lobby . . . doubles are really spacious . . . plenty of furniture . . . large windows . . . large tub and bidet . . . . She looked up. "Which one do you think?"

He looked across the street at each of the hotels. They were both four– or five–storied buildings with balconies from the front rooms. Between the two buildings were a furrier's and an office–machines store. The hotel on the left was newer, but looked like painted cardboard; the other was a grey–stone facade with scrolled iron balconies. "The ironmongers'," he said. "We have enough traveler's checks?"

She tucked the guidebook back into the market basket she had bought in Marlborough, how many Spanish–French–Italian policemen ago, flagging him down with their miniature stop signs like popsicles in their hands and then, when they saw his California license plates, waving him abruptly on as if he had somehow cheated them. It had been that kind of a trip.

"Of course," she said. "Don't be silly." They got out of the car. "Aren't you going to take the bags?"

He slam–locked the car door on his side. "I want to see whether this place is anything more than a back bedroom made over into a hotel," he said, "before I start lugging the luggage."

She smiled, to console him for his stumbling wit, he supposed, as much as for anything else, and took his hand as they crossed the street between traffic to the hotel. Inside the entrance, a red–carpeted staircase went up a flight of steps. Separated by a glass door to the left, was the bar. Thugs in business suits sat on a few of the bar stools, drinks before them. No one was at the two tables near the front window. The bartender had door–width shoulders. The blue–gold monogram $\mathcal{R}$ of the hotel, blurred with dirt, was woven into the carpet at the foot of the stairs. He had the impression that the Pentelic marble had been shunted elsewhere.

In the lobby, no larger than a bedroom at the top of the stairs, the man behind the desk had a black mustache as neat as if painted on his face; his smile had appraised them already, addingmachine quick: travelers; middle–aged; Hush–Puppies; on the road a long time; seeped down from the glass–door foyers of Syntagma Square. Behind him, crowding him, the space was so narrow, were two tiers of mail boxes for ten rooms. Only one key was missing. The lobby entrance stopped abruptly at the end of the desk in a ceiling–to–floor and wall–to–wall mirror. To add depth, he supposed, even though there seemed little purpose in duplicating the acanthus potted in a corner, or the bench opposite the desk, or themselves either. Inset in the mirror–wall was a door, that a mirror too, with a crack from the brass doorknob up to the opposite corner. It was a cartographed, unexplored river. The whole place had the atmosphere of a Victorian water closet disguised behind the facade of a wood–burning stove. He wouldn't have been surprised if the potted acanthus were somehow a cigarette lighter.

"You want a room," the clerk said. It was a statement, not a question. He was pretending to page through a ledger to see what vacancies he had. From outside, up the carpeted staircase behind them, came the noise of traffic whicking past.

"Yes," Cathy said. "We just got in town."

It was a bar stool behind the counter on which the man sat, and his cuff links were silver medallions with owl impressions. A ring the size of an aggie on the hand across the open pages of the ledger implied he might be the heir of the Mycenae treasures. "You plan to stay long?"

"We'll see," he said, looking at the ledger too, pretending to fix in there the quality of the room that would decide just how long it would be.

"Yes, we do have one," the clerk announced as if by white-sale chance they had come exactly when they had. "With breakfast?" The clerk talked to Cathy as if she, the wife, made all the responsible decisions. But he had circumvented that nonsense before. "No," he said. "No breakfast."

The clerk hesitated a moment in deference to what Cathy might say. She said nothing. The registry card was placed in the middle of the counter (he was almost sure now it was a section of the bar from downstairs when the mirrors and the remodeling for the tourists had been done), and he signed their names, took out their passports, and shoved them with the card toward the clerk, "How much will it be?" he asked him—clerk, manager, bellboy, custodian. Hell, he could have been all of them. He probably was.

But the clerk had his own devices—a long study of

something beneath the counter (his cup of coffee slid out of sight when he saw them coming across the street?) as if the complex pricing of hotel rooms engaged Euclidean concepts. "Your room, the one on the second floor with the balcony facing the Acropolis, without breakfast, hot and cold running water, air conditioning optional—200 drachma." They were nice kids, he implied, and deserved the best the Greek tourist office had to offer.

He turned to Cathy. "You want to look at it?"

She shook her head, admitting that the potholes from Patras, the rip–rap over which the sea spray splashed onto their windshield as they went through the little fishing towns, the worrybeads hanging in bunches at the peripteros at Corinth had been enough for that day. "Just get the bags," she said; "my little one and the vanity case for now."

He descended the carpeted stairs toward the street as the clerk coming from behind the desk with the key of the room was saying to Cathy, "I'll show, madam . . . ."

He waited on the curb in front of the hotel while a cluster of cars came with a roar down the one–way narrowness of Metropoleos as if the stoplight at the Square were flushing them down a sewer pipe. Above the tiered houses and shops of the Plaka, however, the sun rested on the buildings of the Acropolis—a cornice here, a column there, telling the shopkeepers it was time to tally up the day's graces.

He brought the bags back to the hotel lobby and set them down before the mirrored wall. His own figure, duplicated, bowed to him, stood upright—a middle–aged man in a tan raincoat, slightly large for him without its inner lining. The clerk was gone. In the building, somewhere behind the wall were the clankings of an elevator, and eventually that portion of the cracked mirror which was the door swung open. It was the clerk, who helped him stack the bags on one side of the elevator (a one–seater outhouse his father would have assessed it), and closed the flexible iron grille for him. "On the second floor," the clerk said. Outside the diamond–bar apertures of the grille his face, the smile, evoked reminiscences of a zoo before the door closed upon it.

He pressed the #2 button and ascended, stopped, pulled the grille back and held it open with his foot while he pushed a bag in front of it. He opened the door to the dimness of a cave, pulled the luggage into the corridor. At the end of the hall, in an open door, stood the figure of Cathy. "Down here," she said.

Bags in hand, he went toward her—past the smell of the public lavatory, layered beneath a wax–coating of Lysol, past the recessed dark doors of other rooms, past a TV set on spindly legs pushed against the end wall of the corridor.

"It's no parador at Javea," she said as she preceded him into the room. She was right. An electric cord from the hall snaked under the closed door to a double socket beneath the light switch on the wall. Between the foot of the twin beds and a wardrobe a gangplank passage led to the windows of the balcony. Cathy had already opened them and the cool air from outside had edged, amoeba like, into the moldiness and grit of the room. "It's really pretty awful," she said.

He put the bags on a table beside the wardrobe and went to the balcony. A half inch of rain water trapped within its rim had made it into an atrium footbath with a terrazza bottom. The rusty mouth of a drainage hole at one end, near the building, had the appearance of having been clogged a long time ago. On the iron balustrade shared with the balcony of the room next door were draped a man's ribbed undershirt and a pair of green socks drying in the sun. As a warning, he tipped one of the socks backward off the balustrade onto its own balcony, and turned back to Cathy, searching her face.

"Well?"

She had her suitcase on the bed, unlocking it. "Let's stay here for tonight. Is that all right?"

He walked past her toward the door at the room's other end. "What's the bathroom like?"

"It could be worse," she said.

Inside, he doubted it. Even with the double windows pushed open onto the black–grey bricks of an airshaft, the room smelled as if it were sitting on the edge of the town's cloaca. He pulled the chain, without a handle, of the overhead W. C. and the water hesitated, slid, gurgled in its pipe, to emerge in a swirl of nonconviction below. In pulling, he had cut his finger on a broken link of the chain—a small smudge of red. He dabbed the cut with his handkerchief. The benefits of tetanus. The washbasin had a central curved spout like those for washing hair in old–fashioned barbershops, and a glass shelf below the mirror had a corner missing like a grey–green, sheered–off glacier. When he turned on the hot–water faucet, he really didn't expect anything to happen. The trickle that came seemed the end of a thousand mile journey from a Carpathian run–off. Hot and cold—crap. He turned off the faucet and came back to Cathy hanging up her two good blouses in the wardrobe.

"I think we'd better keep most of our stuff in the suitcases," she said. She had spread some old maps on the wardrobe shelves, and her purse stood tentatively on one of them like a can of paint on a drop cloth.

He went to the balcony again, to its rain–water footbath, his Hush–Puppies teetering on the rim. Over the balcony, below, was the circled island of parked cars, the Tom–Mix whiteness of his own VW tethered at the curb. The light, afternoon filtered, came around the bulk of the cathedral, whose shadows—a wedge, a block, an ellipsoid—lay against the store fronts opposite as if imposing on the noise of the cars, on the taxi–driver polishing his fender with a fan–dance duster of feathers, even on the blue traffic sign along the curb, the immutable geometric forms. With the water off the balcony, at least they could sit out there in the evening.

He turned back to where Cathy trying to hang up her good blue suit was bumping elbows against the doors of the wardrobe that from either side kept closing in on her like a clam. "Is there an old hanger in there?" he said, coming up beside her.

She handed him one, its hook twisted over like the wrung neck of a bird. "Nothing but," she said.

"I'll see whether I can unplug the drain so we can sit outside." He unbent the hanger, and one foot tiptoeing in the water, he leaned down, jabbing the end of the hanger into the drainage hole. It was useless, as if someone had sealed up the other end with a cork. He came back inside. The waterline across the end of his Hush–Puppies looked as if he were wearing toe rubbers.

Cathy had finished unpacking, had stowed her suitcase on top of the wardrobe, and sat now on the edge of her bed, the uncertain railing of a fence, paging through the guidebook for a place to eat. He stood before her, looping the hanger into wastebasket size.

"Some place with flaming souvlakia, retsina, and a tub of Greek salad," he said. He went to the bathroom, to a wastebasket no larger than a toilet–paper roll, got rid of the hanger, looked, out of curiosity, down the well of the airshaft where it ended in the circled–top of an oildrum against one brick wall, and came back to sit beside Cathy on the bed. "The tambouri weigh approximately . . . ." He pretended to be reading from Mr. Philadelpheus's *Monuments of Athens* that he had paged through on the way over on the ferry.

"You want to eat at the Vassilis or the Corfu?" she said, holding a finger at a back page, the book on her lap.

". . . Pericles in 447 commissioned Ictimus . . . and above the triglyphs and the metopes reigns a row of pearls, the astragali . . . ."

"They're both just across Syntagma Square. You have a preference?" Sitting beside her, he realized as he had before what kind of polestar she was for him, what affection had accumulated in layer after layer of admission that without her he would be little more than a hull, masts broken, lurching into and out of wave troughs.

"The one whose donkeys were shot on the wharves at Smyrna," he said.

She was jotting down an address from the book on a slip of paper. "We'll go to the Corfu," she said. She encircled a sentence in the book: ". . . satisfying though not distinguished."

"Exactly."

"Come on," she said, getting up, tucking the slip of paper into her purse. She went over and closed the windows on the balcony, shutting off the noise of the cars below. "Tomorrow we'll find another place to stay."

Downstairs, when he opened the elevator door onto

the lobby, the clerk behind the counter put down his cigarette as they approached. His smile opened like a sea anemone. "Is Kriesotou Street on the other side of the Square?" Cathy asked him.

"Yes, yes," he said too quickly. "You want a taxi?" His hand hovered over the phone on the counter beside him as if his brother were just around the corner.

"No," she said. "We want to see your city. We'll walk."

He himself stopped for a moment as he shoved the key across the desk. "The balcony's got about an inch of rain water on it. Do you think you could get it fixed?"

"Your room?" It was as if he could not believe such a thing were possible.

"No, the balcony outside the room," he said carefully, and the clerk's smile tightened for the first time. "It's not much," he added. He held his thumb and forefinger apart to show him. "About that much. An inch or so. On the balcony." Cathy had gone down the steps and was waiting below, before the outside entrance. "Twenty–four," he repeated for the clerk. He turned over the identifying plaque of the key as if the guy were having difficulty with English. "That room." He pointed to the number on the plaque. "Two—four." As he talked, the clerk was assessing him again, the eyes like the flat impersonal ends of a binocular, and he himself felt the smile that had vanished from the face in front of him spreading across his own lips. "We'd like to sit out there to view the Acropolis," he said.

The Greek doubted it. "I'll have it fixed right away," he said.

"The drain. At the side . . ."

"I'll have it fixed," the clerk said, turning to deposit the key in its cubicle behind him.

"Thanks," he said, and he went to join Cathy at the bottom of the stairs.

"What was that all about?" They went out to the Athenian evening, cool now, the sun down. The guide-books were right—the air, purple–grey, was as palpable as water around the cornice of a cathedral across the street. Single file on the narrow sidewalk, they started up Mitropoleos toward the Square.

"I just brought him a warning from Delphi," he said, "about watching which way the water flows," but a battery of cars coming down the street, bunched as if on a racetrack, buried his words beneath the whickering of their tires and the snarl of gear–shifting.

Cathy turned her head toward him, over her shoulder, smiling, although she hardly could have heard what he said, and he followed her up from the underground. Or was it supposed to be she following him?

When they returned to the hotel, the smell of the vine leaves from the dolmades hovering around his head, a woman in a tight black skirt was behind the counter on the bar stool. A cigarette canted from the ashtray beside her. The fingers had accumulated rings like barnacles. He was beginning to believe, as reputed, that those polished white statues, those white heads with noses missing, had been gilded with reds and purples, banded with gold.

"Twenty–four," he told her, and she turned around, her hand hesitating a moment before the tier of boxes, and got his key and put it on the counter. Cathy was already at the elevator, her finger on the button.

"We fixed the balcony," the girl said as if to cover up the medieval clanking of chains and shifting of weights going on behind the mirrored wall. She had picked up her cigarette, and the smoke arose before her face like a votive offering. The meticulous sweeps of her black hair could have been carved.

"Thanks," he said. "That'll be fine."

In the corridor upstairs the TV set was on, the picture so fuzzy he couldn't tell whether it was Gary Cooper or Doris Day riding the horse, and the girl across the hall, her door open, sat in the corridor on a stool, watching. He smiled a greeting of some sort as they passed in front of the crossed legs. She looked up from the set, nodded her head. But Mr. Cooper (it was his hat, not Miss Day's) turned the face back toward the grey glow of the screen.

Behind the closed door of their room, he flicked the switch on the wall, but instead of the overhead light going on, he heard the hoofbeats of the TV fade outside. He flicked the switch once more, and the pistol shots began ringing again in the corridor. "Lovely, mirrored lobby . . ."

Cathy had opened the windows and had gone out to the balcony, her hand on the railing. Seen in the frame of the windows, she was a figure beneath the lintel of a stele, so that without pausing to take off his coat, he joined her on the balcony, his arm around her shoulder. "It's been a long, tour-group day," he said.

She didn't turn her head. Above the black bulk of the Plaka, some technician with floodlights was *luminiering*, one by one, the buildings on the Acropolis. The sound was elsewhere.

"That was good souvlakia, wasn't it?" she said.

He acknowledged once again what he had discovered before when the car coughed and stopped in Ubeda, when the rain slashed at the shutters in Sagris, when the mist in Milan never let up—how fortunate he had been to find her amidst the shining hair and smooth limbs of the high–school harem where he had first seen her. "Uncomplaining traveler," he told her.

"Well, it was," she said.

"My napkin was so wet and cold it could have been dried in the refrigerator."

"And to wad it up in the breadbasket?"

"It helped."

"Tomorrow we'll get another place," she said as if she knew the hotels in Athens as well as her own knitting patterns.

Below them he searched out the white top of his VW; it was a pale pool in the Boetian gloom. Above the Plaka the blue–white banks of lights on the #3 *luminiere* panel lit up the east facade of the Parthenon for tour group #71, #106, #2532.

In the morning when he went to shave, the hot–water faucet, when he turned it on, gave no water at all, only a garbled message of thumpings along distant pipes—someone talking from the engine room of a ship. He listened attentively hoping the sounds would come closer. Instead, they faded out into a dying SOS. He shaved in the trickle of the other faucet. The slow stream implied that Aesop tortoises also won races, even though with each stroke he had to wipe his razor clean with a piece of toilet paper.

When he came from the bathroom, Cathy was sitting up in bed, encircling on their Athens map four–starred, not–to–be–missed immensities. "We can't get to the Acropolis from this side," she said, "unless we walk up through the Plaka. If we take the car . . . let's see . . . this is a one way street, and if we go up one more to Ermou . . . ."

"Let's walk," he said. "After all, Diogenes . . . ."

She folded the map in consent and put it on the

night table beside her. "Is there enough hot water for a shower?"

He had gone to the windows of the balcony. Outside, the pair of socks on the balustrade were brown this morning, and in the sunlight instead of the undershirt there were paisley–patterned shorts. He turned to where she sat on the edge of the bed bending to put on her slippers.

"Are you kidding?"

"Isn't there?" She had slimmed to a paradigm as she pushed an arm into her robe and getting up belted it around her waist.

He motioned with his head toward the laundry on the balustrade. "If there ever was, which I doubt, some Anna Livia next door has already used it."

She came over to the window beside him. "Now if you had a wife like that . . . ." She opened the windows and went out to the balcony. The noise of the traffic arose as suddenly as if someone had turned on a radio. He followed her outside, standing beside her, a Prince Phillip, as they addressed the parked cars below. A red VW camper, with beige curtains pulled shut, a circled ⒟ on its back, had managed in the night to squeeze between the taxi–stand and the Mercedes. At the curb it had the tentative appearance of a log ready to be dislodged from the bank of a river. Up the street, he could see just the end of a tour bus pulled up in front of the cathedral. On the Acropolis, the sunlight followed the curves, ran along the gabled lines of the Parthenon, filled up the recesses, warmed the nostrils of the plunging horses at either end of the tympanum. He motioned upward with his head. "Before we look for another hotel?"

Arms upraised, she was taking the bobby pins from her hair, she was putting on a fillet of flowers, the planes of her face steady in the morning light, she was . . . .

"Why don't we?" she said turning back to the room. As he followed her inside, he flipped back the paisley shorts with a finger from the balustrade and they fell in a heap like a dishrag on the floor of the other balcony.

On the Acropolis, the city fallen away on all sides, he felt as if he were standing on the crest of a ring: everything plunged down and away; everything converged to where he stood. No wonder the processions had come winding up from the agora to celebrate here. He had climbed on the ruins—the Parthenon, the Erechtheum, the Propylaea—walking ledges, jumping from step to step, as if exploring an abandoned, half–finished house. Only the Apteros temple, off by itself, an interjected clause, said reflection. He stopped Cathy between its two middle pillars; he unsnapped the case of his best–bargain camera; he took the picture, f–11/125 just before infinity; he buttoned the case back on the camera. "She cannot fade, though thou has not thy bliss . . . ," he said as she came toward him.

"What?" They turned back toward the Parthenon, to the museum behind it.

"A Greek antiphonal," he said. But she ignored him. He helped her up a ledge of rubble, taking her hand. What happened when he was with her was that she deflected everything, like a prism, so that it reached him warm with colors and as varied as he wanted to make it. And it wasn't the shape of the hand in his as he helped her, nor the tug of the fingers as she came up the stepstone of rubble toward him, nor the crown of the head—they were anybody's. So that on the way to the museum as she walked the outside ledge of the Parthenon, he accompanied her a step below, holding his hand upward on which she steadied herself with a touch, walking the rampart past the seventeen pillars with their twenty grooves, their eleven mortised tambouri, their optical options. At the further end, he took both her hands as she jumped to the ground, as she rejoined him.

Inside the museum, before he had entered a step, a guard claimed his camera, a clerk sold him a catalogue. He handed it to Cathy. The entrance way branched off immediately right and left to the galleries. The guard with his taxi–cab cap motioned them to the left. "I'll see you back here," he told Cathy as he went in the opposite direction, to where a statue of Hermes filled the next room.

"All right," she said.

It was his only defense against them: museum guards, gallery guards, garden guards, cathedral guards, cave guards, that he had met from Santillana to Brindisi, from County Sligo to Ravenna—he pretended he didn't understand their directions, even given in English, as if he had come from a colony of Atzugewi Indians isolated so long that only a hundred or so now spoke his language. It was his own gesture of solipsism beside the anonymous mehirs of Carnac that had become, at least for him, almost a necessity.

It was before statue #643 that Cathy later found him. He had come back to it again and again—the head of an archaic Kore among ten or fifteen other fragments, the smile on the lips admitting as one the poppies on the banks of the Aegean, the bowed head under the lintels at Kerameikos, the breaking wave over the thrust of death. He would have liked to talk with the man who had carved it: to find out where he lived, what his wife looked like, how much his olives cost, what alchemy he knew that had changed the daily looks across the harbor into a feminine smile outlasting the noise of Salamis. But someone. Like him. Shaving in cold water.

"Look," he said to Cathy, "I just discovered your portrait."

She glanced once at the Kore. "Not me. I never wore a coronet in my life."

"It has your room number on it, 643."

She stooped to the inscription. "That's at a different hotel," she said.

He let her go then, searching for centaurs, to the next room as if in the crowd of people she were passing him in a tunnel. "There's a girl fastening her sandal in there," he called after her, and she stopped, half–turning at the entrance of the next room. Even after thirty years it was the image of her that recurred—a girl who had been lent to him for a time, a parenthesis of happiness at the edge of another room. "I want you to study the balanced perfection . . . ."

She half raised her hand in a gesture of farewell, and he let her go, cut off by the door jamb of the next room. He went back to the Kore, to the smashed nose which didn't matter, to the holes drilled in the coif for the gold fillet no longer there, to the marble-sealed eyes—all the disjunctives that faded out for the half–parted lips where shadows were light and lights were shadow.

On the way back to the hotel, they stopped at the sidewalk tables outside American Express for coffee, the place a kind of misguided elegance of heavy, silver sugar bowls on sticky metal table tops. The flip–flop seats had been repossessed from a Bijou theater. Across the street, in the Square itself, at other tables, other tourists in mirror–images brought coffee cups to their lips, folded back another page of *Time* magazine. On the left, the facades of the Hotel Bretagne

and the King George with uniformed doormen and
foyers like ballrooms spoke of other Parnassuses.

Cathy was turning the pages of her notebook looking for the Myles King recommendation for an Athens
hotel she had jotted down somewhere. It was these
clues that she had tucked away months ago from talking with strangers at ferry crossings or at Patras cus-
tomhouses that unexpectedly turned into Schliemann
treasures. "Here it is," she said, "the Alkistis Hotel
on the Teatro Placu. Reasonable. Excellent view."

"There isn't an hotel in Athens . . . ." he said.

But she already had her map of Athens out, un-
folded, on the table, trying to read the names printed
on the white tabs of the streets running like wheel
spokes from the center of squares. Watching her bent
head, he knew she warranted more than he could
manage, something out of which fables were born,
instead of the thin, creased packet of traveler's checks
he had for her on which like a raft they had journeyed
so far. On the corner a man sold sponges from a full
net, as big as a buoy; above the trees of the Square
was the unused parliament building where a pair of
Evzones with stamping wooden shoes choreographed
the retreats and advances of warriors long dead; outside the Bretagne a taxi screeched in a quick change
of lanes and pulled up at the curb as if at a pit stop.
What day? What month?

"Here it is," Cathy said, her voice filled with satis-
faction. She turned the map for him to see, her finger-
tip held on the place.

"Next to the stockyards, right?"

"It's over here in back of us," she said. "Off what's
that street . . . Evripidou? By Athinas and Sofokleos."
She bent over the map like a general spotting artillery
targets. "You want to see whether they have a room?"

"Air conditioning optional?"

"It's right over here," she said, her finger attached to the map.

But when they did get there, dodging vegetable carts and three–wheeled trucks hauling barrels of olives, past meat markets with slaughtered lambs hanging upside down, past a row of ten to fifteen shoe–repair cubicles in which men took nails from their mouths and hammered them into soles as if staking down the earth, the manager of the Alkistis from behind his glasses, his finger running down the lines of his ledger, said, "In two days, sir. That's the soonest." He could have been St. Peter with wisps of white hair above his ears. When he, himself, turned to Cathy beside him, the slope of coat beneath the shoulder strap of her bag had already consented.

They made reservations for Friday. They went outside to the polished belt of the guard at the entrance of the police station on the right, to the blue and white sign for tourist parking across the street.

"This'll be fine," Cathy said. "We'll be right next to all the market places."

And they were: the open gunny sacks of beans and moth balls and corn propped up on the sidewalks before the store entrances, the step pyramids of yellow laundry soap, the shoes that looked as if made of cardboard leaning in racks outside against the windows.

"The mysteries of the East," he said as they picked their way across the street. The smells were unseen currents through which like a ship they rode back to their hotel—the dust of granaries, chicken feathers, scabs of blood, rusted barrel hoops, axle–grease, the sun–drenched haunch of a horse standing at a curb.

When they got back to the hotel it was already late in the afternoon. The dust had settled deeper into the nap of the red carpet on the steps to the foyer, and as they came up the stairs, on the waiting bench across from the desk sat what looked like two Pandars talking to the manager. In their dark suits they too gave the impression of cufflink glintings, buffed fingernails.

Without his having to ask, the manager took their key from the tier of boxes and slid it across the counter, as if Greek managers paid special attention to visitors, their names, their wishes, the number of their hotel room.

"*Efcharisto*," he said, as if in turn he immediately was learning the native language without any trouble.

While he and Cathy stood before the mirrored door of the elevator waiting for the clanking of the machinery to stop, it was impossible to avoid the images facing them. His hair had the shaggedness of a highland sheepdog's, winter coming on, and Cathy's low—heel shoes were planted like the feet of a statue on the red plinth of the carpet. The talking of the two on the bench was head—bending discreet. Behind him in the mirror the manager pretended once more to be studying the complicated ledger of reservations he was flooded with.

In their room, Cathy turned back the coverlet on one of the beds for a rest before dinner. He himself pushed the stuffed armchair that belonged in the flea market across the lip of the windows to the balcony outside. The socks, the paisley shorts were gone from the balustrade.

"Close the windows, will you?" From behind him, Cathy's voice came from the curled cocoon of her blanket.

He did, and sat then, his feet on the balcony railing, while the five o'clock coldness filled up the street below him. From a cafe across the street emerged a waiter in a white apron, carrying a circular tray suspended, like a scale of justice, by three—thongs? wires? From that distance, he couldn't tell. On it a glass of water. A white porcelain coffee cup. Shapes in the shadows. The white apron hurried like a messenger boy around a corner into the grey tunnel of a side street and was gone. In the square below, the Ⓓ VW had vanished from the curb.

By Friday when they were ready to leave the hotel, he had learned how to buy airmail stamps at the postal station on Voulis; they had found a coffeehouse where they could get breakfast at eleven o'clock; he had a finger–pointing ritual about candybars with the periptero man at the corner near the hotel; and he had learned a short cut up from Mitropoleos to Cooks where the agents behind the counter looked at him suspiciously, like bank tellers, while he walked past them on his way downstairs for his mail. He could have been home. He had bought himself a pair of worrybeads that he twirled in his hand as he walked past the photographer with his tripod in the Square, as he nodded to a guy selling pistachio nuts.

On the day they left, after he had packed the car, he came back to pay the bill. "Are you leaving town?" The manager spoke while he was going through an elaborate totalling of figures beyond the edge of the counter. The hair of the bent head, black, luxuriant, looked as if it had been chiseled with infinite care.

It was none of his business where they were going. "We thought we might take some side trips," he found himself saying. He remembered Cathy's list: "Delphi, Olympia, Sounion." He made it sound like a trip to Turkey.

"You can have the same room when you come back," the clerk said, looking up, smiling as if it were the best ambassadorial suite he had. None of the sculpture he had seen had bothered to perpetuate that baring of teeth. He said nothing.

92

The clerk returned to his scratch pad. "That was room number twenty–four, right? For three days . . . it comes to 900 drachma."

While he took out his wallet, he tried to remember what the prices posted on the back of the door had been—with air conditioning, without air conditioning; from this summer season to that falling off in the fall. He put the notes on the counter, and waited for the receipt. Apparently there was to be none. As the money disappeared somewhere below the counter, he finally said, "Can I get a receipt?"

On the back of an old calendar slip the manager scrawled in English the amount received and signed his name. It was so illegible it could have been the signature of a Pharoah. He tucked the receipt into his billfold as carefully as if it were his return passage home, but the manager was already lighting another cigarette.

He made one last check of the hotel room. On the notice back of the door was the price: 200 drachma. Times three. He jotted down the address of the National Tourist Agency at the bottom of the notice, went to the bathroom where he turned on the hot water faucet a last time and listened to the thumpings in the pipes below; pulled the broken chain of the water closet; came to the windows of the balcony where outside on the balustrade invisible hands had hung two ribbed undershirts. On the way out of the room he pulled from its socket the cord of the TV set and dropped it on the floor.

Downstairs, as he passed the desk, the manager was reading a paperback. "*Ciaou*," he said to him as he went past just to remind him of Caesar and the Holy Roman Empire to come.

In the car, he told Cathy what had happened. "I think the bastard cheated us a couple hundred drachma." He pulled out of the parking space and into the traffic on Mitropoleos.

"It doesn't make that much difference," she said. "He probably needs the money to fix his hot–water system."

"He hasn't got a hot–water system," he said. He himself hadn't made up his mind what he would do. But the receipt in his pocket was unequivocal enough. As was the address of the government tourist agency: 2 Karageorgi Servias.

Their room at the Alkistis had double twin beds, a balcony with chairs and a table outside for evening quietude facing the Acropolis, and enough hot water to fill the Marathon reservoir. The price was the same. The more he thought about the broken chain of the water closet and the green pair of socks on the balustrade, the more his anger like a headache pressed on his ear drums.

Across the street on a walled rooftop a hundred yards away, an adolescent Greek with a helmet of black hair practiced weightlifting—knee bends, wrist snaps, the works. The sunset made his sloping shoulder glisten in Discobolus dreaming.

Cathy put down her demitasse cup of Turkish coffee on the table between them. "So he overcharged you."

"It's not what I came to Greece for," he said, "to have some owl cufflinks Athena me out of my money."

"He was paying you a compliment. You've obviously got more money than that kid watching TV in the corridor or you wouldn't be traveling in Europe." She was looking over the balustrade toward the covered fruit market at the end of the street.

"Compliment, hell."

She turned to him smiling.

"I mean it."

"Look," she said, nodding over the balcony to the street below. Seven or eight stories down ΔΗΜ ΧΡΥΣΙΝΑΣ (the sign over the shop front said) was turning over with a scoop the olives in the sidewalk barrels lined up in front of his place.

"That's an old Greek trick to keep the rotten ones on the bottom," he said.

"How you talk." She picked up her coffee cup again. "You want to go bull–leaping on Crete for a couple of days?" It was her way to stop his fuming, he knew. "With Viking Tours," she added. "Five days that even we can afford. I looked it up."

On the rooftop the weightlifter had put down his bellbar and changed to soccer. In any case, he was practicing kicks with a ball against one of the roof parapets in a solitary, foot–nimbleness of satyr danc-ing, and, below, ΔΗΜ had gone back inside the en-trance cave of his shop and left the cones of olives glis-tening in the sun. "Of course I want to go to Crete," he said.

He wrote the letter that night. To the Hellenic Tourist Information, Hotel Manager, c/o National Tourist Organisation:

> "This is to file an official complaint with
> your agency against the Hotel Regent,
> 63 Mitropoleos, Athens . . . ."

It was a long letter, specific, detailed, polite . . .

> "If the regulations you establish for the pro-
> tection of tourists in your country are to be
> ignored by hotel managers such as the Hotel
> Regent, perhaps people would be better ad-
> vised to vacation in places other than in
> Greece. I am not interested in causing trouble;
> I am interested, however, in procedures in
> your country whereby visitors know what they
> are paying for and why. Then there will be

no difficulty, and everyone can enjoy the intellectual, aesthetic, and historical interests your country so generously possesses."

He sent a carbon copy to the manager of the Regent Hotel, and went with Cathy to Crete, where the rhython vases and the snake goddesses and the B–P oil tanks all watched the goats nibble on the headlands above the harbor barrios.

When they returned to the Alkistis in five days, his mailbox looked like a magpie nest filled with notes of telephone calls, letters from the Tourist Agency, more telephone calls. He took them to his room and over an ouzo on the balcony sorted them out while Cathy unpacked her dresses. Obviously the manager of the Hotel Regent wanted to talk with him—please call 842–195 as soon as Mr. Lauffer returns. The Tourist Agency letter from Dmitri Some–opolis requested that at his convenience he call at the Agency office for the refund of his money, and that the manager of the Hotel Regent would be . . . shot, he supposed.

He called the Hotel Regent. The barely audible voice was not what he remembered: Yes, the bill was wrong. No, it was an honest mistake. A man would be over in half an hour with his money. They could close his hotel for three months. He would be fined. If Mr. Lauffer would write the Tourist Office, explaining . . . . He saw the ashtray on the hotel desk heaped with cigarette butts, the crack widening in the mirrored door of the elevator, the gritty staircase carpet tumbling step by step toward the street. The silver cufflink holding the phone, waited.

"I wrote the Tourist Agency what happened," he told the silence of the receiver. "It's their problem, now. And yours." He found his voice as he talked assuming all kinds of Draconian impartialities.

"An honest mistake, Mr. Lauffer. All of us . . . sometime . . ."

"Perhaps," he said. He was not above imagining what difficulties lay in keeping clean that mirrored wall for customers to stare at.

"You will write another letter . . . ?"

"If you want me to write them again," he said, "I will, saying you said it was an honest mistake. Then your Agency can decide what should be done." He waited for the voice at the other end to go on, but he heard only the release of a breath, smelled the cigarette smoke as it swirled up from the mouth of the receiver.

"All right, Mr. Lauffer, all right. You won't take the money if I send it over?"

"No," he said, "I don't want the money. I want you to charge the correct price for your rooms."

"I do, Mr. Lauffer, I do," but the voice was as sad as the waves on the rocks below Sounion. "Goodbye, Mr. Lauffer." It was the handwave of one of the kids he was sending to the Minotaur.

"Goodbye," he said, and hung up.

Cathy had come to sit on the edge of the bed. "You got him in trouble, didn't you?" It was as if he had willfully entrapped the guy into overcharging him.

"He got himself in trouble. I had nothing to do with it."

That evening as he knotted his tie for early dinner between the limp collar tabs of his drip–dry shirt, and Cathy did her fingernails, he heard the footsteps in the corridor outside and then the knock on the door. When he opened it, a maid stood there with a tissue–wrapped bunch of flowers as big as a tree in front of her smiling face. "For Mrs. Lauffer," she said, giving him the flowers.

Cathy had come up beside him. "For me?"

"I put them in a vase?" the maid said. Her smile like a beacon had swung from him to Cathy.

"Will you?" Cathy said. She took the flowers from him and gave them back to the maid, who took a small white envelope from the top of the tissue paper and handed it to Cathy. "I get a vase," she said and went back down the corridor.

He closed the door; Cathy opened the envelope. The note was from the manager of the Hotel Regent. She read it and handed it to him as if proving how wrong he had been. "Dear Mrs. Lauffer. An honest mistake, please belief. The Manager, Hotel Regent." It was just gauche enough to ally wives against insane husbands. He tossed the note onto the bed. "He thought a trenchcoat with a zipper lining wouldn't know an Athenian from a Macedonian."

"He thought nothing of the kind," Cathy said. "As he says, he made an honest mistake." A knock at the door told them the maid had returned. In the vase, the flowers, spread out, were even more impressive—roses, lilies, a half dozen carnations. The maid held them out as if presenting a gift of the government.

"*Efcharisto*," he said, and she answered something in Greek and left, her happiness for his wife like a halo following down the corridor above her head.

He brought the vase back to Cathy. She buried her face in the flowers—an image of a St. Blaze blessing. "Aren't they lovely." She set them on the coffee table in front of the balcony windows where in the sunlight they filled the room in a fountain of color. Through them, across them, outside the double, glass–sliding doors, beyond the balcony, he saw the sunlight on the gabled Parthenon where the Kore kids had come bearing gifts, so that when Cathy took his hand and they went to the balcony to watch the last of the day's sunlight, he came like a neophyte given another chance before the akroterion of the temple to understand the immutable pyramids of barrelled olives in the narrow, air–shaft sidestreet seven stories below.

Due Process

Whereas: My wife's voice, answering the telephone, comes to me between long pauses from the other room: "No!" And then later: "When? When did it happen? Yes. Of course. No, he's right here; I'll tell him."

I am correcting bluebooks in my chair beside the living room window. Outside, the ailanthus tree has dropped its leaves yesterday all at once, and the leaves are lying in a circle on the ground now like a veil at its feet. In the light of the November afternoon the trunk stands, all elbows and knees, against the grape–stake palings of the fence. A finch, rose–throated, whets his bill against a top branch as if he too has lost his purpose. The telephone receiver thumps in its cradle, and Cathy comes into the room. "You won't believe this," she says, "but George Holmes is dead. He had a heart attack yesterday in Tucson."

"George? You're kidding."

"That was Jane Pickett. She just heard from Sharon."

"George Holmes?" The anger buried beneath the ashes of five years flares again.

"You better call Alec," she says. And . . .

WHEREAS: The college we had both come to ten years before is on a hilltop facing the ocean, a Pacific still shining in those days like a band of blue silk beyond the fringe of palm trees in the distance. The president rules the college as if it is a fief entrusted to him by the Pope. Before we had come, he has surrounded himself with a cadre of deans—Taylor, Price, Godwin, Allen. Those first years they wear their arrogance like epaulets. But we too had been in the army. We test them with smiles; we bait them with sirs. Emerging from the administration building together at noon, they come in their uniform blue suits across the campus sidewalks toward the cafeteria while we watch from our offices and follow the sphere of their bald heads in the black V of our rifle sights. We speculate. We wait. The possibilities are infinite and appealing.

In May of the second year, the president dismisses without notice a man in psychology—Ellendorf—for suggesting he might be given a better schedule. It is the gambit, the movement in the grass, we have been waiting for. George, I, Bill, Hu, Mike begin our appeals to the faculty organizations, writs to the Academic Senate, letters to the American Association of University Professors in Washington, notes to the legislators to look into the affairs of the college. In the corridors there is a grapevine of plottings in which we suddenly discover comrades we had never known before. The next year George publishes an article in an educational journal called "Handbook for Administrators." It makes fun of them all. We read parts of it, like a manifesto, to each other in our offices. It is the Boy Scout Handbook to study for our first–class badges. And . . .

WHEREAS: The president, having been shown the article by one of his deans, dismisses George, like Ellendorf, without warning. This time it is flagrant enough to get us a legslative hearing before the State Assembly's Educational Committee in Los Angeles. And . . .

WHEREAS: That time, once wave crashing on the shore, has diminished now to a waterline far up on the beach, only a few images remain—one of our play-ing tennis with him those first years on Friday after-noons, our classes over. Four of us play, the bell-wether of George's voice leading us in a file through the gate onto the courts of Recreation Park. Lee Gar-ner and George against Alec and me. We laugh at him; we laugh with him—for the red edge of his underwear hanging down below his white tennis shorts; for the bustle with which he strips the flexible wristwatch band from over his hand and tucks the watch under his towel at the foot of the net post. Alec and I never win even on the balmiest of days when the crowns of the eucalyptus trees beside the courts are bronze–green bouffants against the Palo Verdes hills, and a jet, too distant to be seen, leaves a white curving track across the blue of everywhere.

George's serve is a wobbling slice that drops into corners, followed to the net by a scrambling crisscross-ing of knees, by a red–edged bagginess of shorts. His forehand is a drop–shot that he punches toward lines, angles over the net, dribbles off into a vacated valley. His backhand arcs over our heads in perpetual lobs to fall a few inches inside the baseline.

By the end of the first set I am yelling for Alec to crowd the net, not to crowd the net; to counter–lob, not to counter–lob; to play Garner's backhand—to do the impossible. George is like a shadow, there before we have made up our minds to hit the ball to where he already waits. He bustles around the net when we ex-change sides, squinting up at the sun, testing the wind with a wet finger.

"Cut it out, George," I tell him as I pass, taking the balls proffered me on his racket. "There isn't any wind and you know it."

A smile slides across his mouth as he walks to his side of the court, an exaggerated puppet who had he played with a bow tie on above his T–shirt no one would have been surprised. He returns my best serves, lunging to retrieve them, scarcely getting his racket on the ball which educated, erratic, flops over Alec's head at the net or bloops off the wood in a carom of correctness. It is only after he has been fired, when he comes back summers from his teaching in Arizona, skin tautened like an Indian's, that going to the courts once more in a gesture of continuity, do Alec and I manage to win. The élan is gone, the strut collapsed into a slow walk to the baseline as he gets ready to serve. Because written over the green clumps of the tree–heads like sky writing for everyone to see is the fact of his dismissal. We pretend not to notice. But the banter has stopped, and only occasionally, when the intervening year has dissolved in the sunshine, does his serve come in at all. The red shorts are gone.

Later, after Alec has won the set for us with one of his sliced forehand drives, like a ping–pong shot, to the far alley, we sit on the green bench beside the court, towelling the sweat from our faces.

"Lucky Alec," George says. "Lucky Alec." But he doesn't care. He plays with us now because he wants to talk, not about tennis but about us, about the college that is going to, that must, rehire him just to wipe the stigma from his name. His blue eyes search each of us for a chink, for an outcropping to help him up the mountain his dismissal has become for him. And for us too, I realize, sitting beside him.

"How about it, Lauffer?" he says, turning to me. "You heard from AAUP yet?" I had been president of the local chapter the year after he had been fired, and my files are thick with letters of inquiry, of politeness, and finally of frustration against the answers which sound like the exchanges of a ladies' embroidery circle. What those signatures said in dribbles of apprehension was that Holmes's case was very serious they thought, but for now, however . . . . What the letters said was they wished George would somehow vanish.

I stuff my towel into my bag and toss my racket on the ground beside it.

"No, I haven't heard, George."

"Why not, Lauffer?"

"Don't ask me," I say without looking at him. "I've mailed you a copy of every letter I've sent them. You know what I've said—'when the hell are we going to get our Committee A for George Holmes?' "

Alec still stands at the net leaning on the round head of the post. He has a wife and three daughters and his tennis is wedged between babysitting and taking out the laundry. His first inclination is kindness. In my saner moments I admire him for it. At other times, he just seems obtuse. "But didn't their last letter mention something about Committee A in the fall?" he says.

"Come on, Alec," I say sharply. "They've been promising that for a year and nothing has happened. You know that as well as I do."

"What if I wrote them again?" George says to me.

With the toe of my tennis shoe I am scrubbing out a caravan of ants hustling along a crack in the cement underneath the bench. "It can't do any harm," I tell him.

"And you, Lauffer?" It is a shove.

"All right; I'll write them again." And . . .

WHEREAS: That summer diminishes to fall and George goes back to Arizona in his green Volkswagen sedan, pulling away from my curb after our goodbyes, rolling up the window, his blue, polka–dot tie a pennon of hope against the three–hundred miles of desert driving ahead of him. He still keeps his home in town, his wife and daughter there—a harbor he would return to.

He comes back at Christmas, and Alec and I and Garner have breakfast together one morning at a pancake house on Pacific Coast Highway—to go through the gesture of re–establishing a time that all of us know will never be put together again. We pull up our chairs around the table and glance at the fifty different varieties of pancakes that someone has thought up. Across the table from me, the cheeks that before have been pink are broken–veined now as if the skin has grown tired and thinned, and the eyes go backward behind the circles of flesh like thumbprints into dough. The bow tie, this one red, seems longer, its ends sharper, its knot wrinkled tight. Around him has settled an aura of weariness, and in the ridges fanning out from the corners of his eyes to his temples run the white lines of concrete and the billows of 95 degree heat of Highway 66 from Barstow to Needles across the Mojave to Arizona.

The heavy–thick table in front of us with its coppice of syrup bottles, the stolid captain chairs, spindled and ugly in which we sit, even the black and white checkered hats of the chefs behind the waist–high kitchen counter, seem unnecessarily gross as we examine once more the problem of George Holmes, a blueprint on the table before us. But it is an act, and all of us know it, because we have dug in sand before to know how the first wave crumbles the edges of our parapets and how the snicker of the second will wash over us so that, glanced at, we will be no more than a scallop's infringement on the flat, wet glimmer of the beach.

Alec has taken my place as president of the AAUP chapter, but it doesn't matter who has the title; we are all encircled. I study the menu while George shoves questions at us as if he is loading the belt of a machine gun. On the menu are buckwheat cakes, and Silver

Dollars, and Uncle Tom's Special with Applesauce, and Blueberry Delights, and the Chef's Choice with Three Strips. I flip–flop through the front and back of the menu, the columns, the outlined boxes, the *à la carte* coynesses.

"But I did, George," Alec is saying. "I did. I sent the last letter only a week ago."

"But why not again, Alec?" It is a bluntness without the amenity of a smile, the offering of a cigarette.

I close the menu and push it to the center of the table. "We have, George; we all have." The water glasses are tumblers with fluted sides and as heavy as grenades. I take a drink and return the glass to the paper placemat in front of me—a map of California dotted with towns in which other hopeless men all through the state are eating the Chef's Special. George looks at me as if I were someone he had forgotten about, an overcoat bumped into by chance in the closet in the middle of a hot summer.

"I know," he says. "Will once more hurt you?"

There is no answer to that. Nothing helpful at least. I sip my water; I return the glass to its map of California. "Those bastards," I say, and everyone knows whom I mean. It is the weather–vane turning we do, pointing our frustrations in one direction, which we use to make us friends again, phalanxed against those who had started it a long time ago and who, we imagine, sit now in the evenings before their fireplaces, unwitting, immune. Some have already resigned, emeritus, from the college—like the president, his commissioned portrait–in–oil gracing the wall behind the information desk in the main office. Whenever I want to get angry, I walk past it to remind myself—of him, of George, of us, of me.

We cut through his grossness with our forks in the layered pancakes sodden with syrup in the plate before us. We dump invectives upon the deans as we shake the sugar into our coffee. It keeps us from saying what we have come not to say—that except for three or four of us George Holmes is gone from the college, no longer of much concern to it—gone along with the red–plush rocking chair he had furnished his office with, along with his voice ricocheting through the corridors and against our half–open doors. And . . .

WHEREAS: I am in Alec's study at his home, the last AAUP letter he has got from the national office in my hand. "Damn it, Alec, stop asking them; tell them. This is the third year, and all we have is another letter, another excuse." I toss the letter back beside his type-writer onto the desk. "You know where that'll get George." I have had my turn the year before. I can direct my anger at him now.

Alec turns around from his desk. Behind him in an apple tree out the window a hummingbird hovers at the tip of a tube filled with red, sugared water. "What else do you want me to do? I've already written them three times in two months." His own anger with me tightens around the words.

"You want me to write them?" It is a phrase, a bravado. He knows it is. I know it is.

"What the hell good would that do?" He picks up the letter and reads it through again. "All right," he says. "I'll write them once more." And . . .

WHEREAS: My olive tree in the spring, wind tossed, turns upward its grey-green leaves, and sitting in my chair near the window I watch my daughter, at eighteen, sitting on the floor cutting out of white construction paper silhouettes of a handclasp—for post-ers, I think. For some week at her high school. For some something. Scattered around her are a few of the finished placards—a black hand encircling a white one, a white one around a black, in a yang–yin picture of what looks to me like the intertwined wires of an electrical circuit. "What's that?" I ask her. The question is directed toward the top of her bent head. I don't expect an answer, but neither do I want to begin sorting out just then the debris left of George Holmes from the two years we have spent trying to get him back.

She answers without looking up, her elbow askew as she uses the scissors around a curved line of the paper. Her blonde hair, caught in a bandolier behind her ears, waterfalls across her shoulders. She is wearing a dark blue sweatshirt with the word D Y N A M I C embroidered in a column like a caryatid down the back. The name is a high–school club. I know that much. "They're for AFS," she says. She places the cut–out silhouette on the sheet of another poster, centers it, arranges it. And then, mucilage applied to the back of the paper, she thumps it with a fist onto the poster, prints April 11–18 under the silhouette, and puts the poster aside.

I return to my window, to the far corner of my patio where an old–fashioned porch swing holds still in the lath–striped sunshine of the afternoon, to the red, heavy–headed blooming of the bottlebrush against the further fence, to the nandina crowding the ferns in that shadow's quiet. And you, George Holmes, in Arizona, what now? What charging to the net in your red–edged shorts do you do on that cracked adobe?

It is you, he says. I was only the hone. It is you who need the answers, not me. How much I meant to you in Room 302 of the L. A. courthouse that day in November where I sit before the Assembly Committee uncovering, as one of the legislators said, the worst mess in education he had encountered in twenty years on the committee. That—to find out for you in answering them how much you know of yourself. Because it is for you the benefits have accrued—the president forced to resign; your desk orderly with aligned books in your office now; the view toward the ocean from your third–floor window interrupted only by a palisade of palms like inverted feather dusters against the horizon. Legacy. From me to you. And in the last few years, perhaps a paratrooper feeling of toughness about you for belonging to that time of George Holmes. That too perhaps from me like a battle ribbon, like a gold, over-seas stripe you can affix to the sleeve of your jacket. For you, because of me.

I return to my daughter, to where she picks up the pile of posters, the scissors, the pot of paste, and goes from the room, the edge of the doorway like the case-ment of a window shutting her abruptly off, a bird that has winged through my house a moment, in one window out another, and then is gone. As she will be. So that I listen intently as if to engrave into perma-nence the sound of her telephone dialing in the other room, the click, the returning whir, the click, and her voice then, in love: "Tim? When you bring . . . ." And . . .

WHEREAS: George comes back for the third summer, and the day he returns I find myself riding with him in his Volkswagen downtown. We stop at Ryan's, the Volkswagen dealer, because the gasket in the cap of the gasoline tank is leaking. And when he lifts the hood to show the repairman, I see the flat cardboard box of grapefruit he has brought back, three or four dozen, yellow and shining in the cave of his trunk, and I begin to divide three years into forty grapefruit, to assess the dividend of that reward—364 x 3 divided by forty—to tabulate the compensa-tions that have fallen his way. "The head of the de-partment gave them to me," he says, but I don't know whether he is joking or not.

110

The repairman gets the gasket, fits it in the cap, tightens the cap back on the tank, and closes the lid of the trunk on the grapefruit. It isn't until we are on Pacific Coast Highway on the way home, the six lanes of traffic flowing with little more than a hesitation at the stop lights, that he speaks again. "You're not on the Executive Board either this year, are you?"

I admit I am not.

"You don't know what the chapter is doing?" It isn't a question, for the voice is already keyed toward what he knows I will say.

"No. The accreditation report was the last I heard."

We drive in silence, his head and shoulders, as immobile as a portrait, fixed above the steering wheel. When we get caught by the traffic light at Redondo and he shifts into neutral, his hand still resting on the knob of the shift, he speaks once more, even yet not looking at me. But the hand next to my knee is not just anyone's hand, but his. I know that much. "It isn't any use, is it?"

I hesitate: "What isn't any use?"

"Me," he says. "Trying to get me back on the faculty." The red brake lights of the Pontiac station wagon in front of us fade out, and George shifts into first, following the square tailgate across the intersection. When he shifts into second, he looks at me for the first time. "Is it?"

It has been three, long, abrasive years. "Not now," I admit. It isn't what I want to say, but at least I can be that honest with him and the four dozen grapefruit in the trunk ahead of us. Below us Pacific Coast Highway dips to a traffic circle, and in the distance to the left near a shopping center a small Ferris wheel turns, and a merry–go–round no larger than a doughnut lies in a corner where two streets meet. Beyond is the green water tower of the Veterans' Hospital and next to that, I know, is the college, and beyond that beneath a maze of telephone poles and half–grown acacia trees is the place, indistinct and buried, where I live, fence–bound, and two or three blocks of nonentity further is the house where George's family still lives.

We swoop down the hill toward the traffic circle, merge momentarily with the inner lanes, and then tack off on an exit to the other side, the highway ahead cutting straight before us through the clusters of buildings toward Seal Beach, Surfside, Huntington, Corona del Mar, San Diego. But instead of turning left at Ximeno to take me home, he keeps on Seventh to where the college sits on its hill looking at the Pacific. I know why he has brought me here, but I don't mind. It seems fitting enough. He turns in the college gates and drives slowly through the campus—down East College Drive, along Atherton, up West Campus Road, past the blue–panelled facade of the administration building as if taking me on a tour. As we pass the new, five–story audio–visual building, he bends his head to look out the windshield. "A year ago," I say as if admitting to a fault.

Farther on he points to the intaglio impressed across the wall of the new Fine Arts Building. "Just this spring," I say. "Two–hundred thousand dollars." We have made the circuit and are back on Atherton where the portico of the Physical Education complex is a black pencilled fracturing of light against panels of glass three stories high and a football field long.

"I remember . . . ," he begins, but he has no intention of finishing the sentence. He will let me do that, the tour finished, having yoked us—him, me, the college, the grapefruit in the trunk—one last time; and I think for a moment that there probably had been nothing wrong with the gasket in the first place, that he had raised the hood of the trunk knowing I would be there

112

to let me see what we had left him from our times together.

He drops me off at the curb in front of my house. I close the door of the car and reaching through the open window shake his hand. "We'll see you, George. How long will you be in town?" With the clutch in, he is revving the motor.

"I don't know," he says. "A week. Perhaps ten days." Beyond his face, across the street, is the battered aluminum garbage can that has been left by the neighbors from yesterday's pickup, and behind me I hear the belly–flopping splash of Randy, the kid next door, in his swimming pool.

"Perhaps Alec?" I say.

He looks at me as if he has never heard the name before. "Alec?"

"Or Hu. He'll be president of the Academic Senate next year."

George shifts into first and makes a little gesture of farewell, of dismissal really. "So long," he says.

THEREFORE: Even though it is November and the leaves are gone from my ailanthus tree, I do not call Alec to tell him George is dead. Nor do I call Hu. Nor Mike. Nor Bill. It is a temptation I owe George not to take. What is to be left me now and then when I raise the hood of my own Volkswagen will be a mound of gleaming grapefruit that I will be trying to cover over with two canvas backrests for the beach, or the six–plaque section of straw mat that is to be taken to my mother–in–law in Claremont when we go next time, or the cracked tarpaulin I use when I haul firewood home from Zempke's Lumber Company on B Street in Wilmington.